# The Hunted Heart

## A Redwood Pack Novella

By
CARRIE ANN RYAN

ISBN-13: 978-1-943123-33-9

Cover Art by Charity Hendry

# The Hunted Heart

Emeline might have been alive hundreds of years, but she's never really lived. Using her knowledge and research, she helped save the Redwood Pack from devastation. However, she's never felt whole. Not since she lost her mate so long ago. Now there is a new, younger wolf, entering her life and it will take more than her nose in a book to figure out the warmth in her heart is much more than a promise of a new feeling. It's fate.

Noah has known Emeline was his mate since he first saw her, only he doesn't know if she feels the same. He's always been on the fringes of those in power in the Pack and has enjoyed it. Now he's become an integral piece and wants to find a way to bring Emeline with him. Her reluctance in dating a much younger wolf isn't the only hurdle in his way.

When he finally takes the step, he'll have to pray she finds the connection and lets fate save them both. As they find their way to a mating bond, a player from the past is out to hold them back and everything they thought they'd had might be lost forever.

Dedication

For those who begged me for
a ‘cougar’ story.

# Redwood Pack Characters

With an ever growing list of characters in each book, I know that it might seem like there are too many to remember. Well don't worry; here is a list so you don't forget. Not all are seen in this exact book, but here are the ones you've met so far. As the series progresses, the list will as well.

Happy reading!

**Adam Jamenson**—Enforcer of the Redwood Pack, third son of the Alpha. Mate to Bay and father to Micah. Story told in *Enforcer's Redemption* and *Forgiveness*.

**Anna Jameson**—late mate of Adam.

**Bay Jameson**—new member of the Redwood Pack. Mate to Adam and mother to Micah. Story told in *Enforcer's Redemption* and *Forgiveness*.

**Beth**—member of the Redwood Pack. Aunt to Emily.

**Brie Jamenson**—daughter of Jasper and Willow.

**Cailin Jameson**—Only daughter of Edward and Pat. Mate to Logan. Story told in *Fighting Fate*.

**Camille**—deceased former member of the Redwood Pack.

**Caym**—demon from Hell summoned by the Centrals. Lover of Corbin.

**Charlotte Jamenson**—half-sister of Ellie's. Will be raised as a daughter by Ellie and Maddox.

**Conner Jamenson**—son of Josh, Reed and Hannah. Twin to Kaylee.

**Corbin Reyes**—new Alpha of the Central Pack. Lover of Caym.

**Cyrus Ferns**—deceased former unit teammate of Josh's.

**Donald**—member of the Redwood Pack.

**Edward Jamenson**—Alpha of the Redwood Pack. Mate to Pat.

Father to Kade, Jasper, Adam, Reed, Maddox, North and Cailin.

**Ellie Jameson**—Daughter of the former Alpha of the Central Pack. Mate to Maddox and mother to Charlotte. Story told in *Shattered Emotions*.

**Emily**—young member of the Redwood Pack. Orphan and niece of Beth.

**Emeline**—elder of the Redwood Pack. Lost her mate in the first war with the Centrals.

**Finn Jameson**—son of Kade and Melanie. Future Heir and Alpha of the Redwood Pack.

**Franklin**—deceased former member of the Redwood Pack. Camille's lover.

**Gina Jamenson**—newly adopted daughter of Kade and Melanie. Her birth parents, Larissa and Neil were killed during an attack.

**Hannah**—Healer of the Redwood Pack. Mate to Josh and Reed. Mother of Conner and Kaylee. Story told in *Trinity Bound* and *Blurred Expectations*.

**Hector Reyes**—deceased former Alpha of the Central Pack. Father to Corbin, Ellie, Charlotte and Ellie's twin.

**Henry**—Redwood Pack member and store owner for 60 years.

**Isaac**—deceased member of the Central Pack.

**Jason**—member of the Redwood Pack and one of the Alpha's enforcers.

**Jasper**—Beta of the Redwood Pack. Mate to Willow and father of Brie. Story told in *A Taste for a Mate* and *A Beta's Haven.*

**Jim**—hot dog vendor and one of Josh's former friends.

**Joseph Brentwood**—deceased former Alpha of the Talon Pack.

**Josh Jamenson**—former human Navy Seal. A Finder and

partial demon. Mated to Reed and Hannah. Father to Conner and Kaylee. Story told in *Trinity Bound* and *Blurred Expectations*.

**Kade Jamenson**—Heir and future Alpha of the Redwood Pack. Mate to Melanie. Father to Finn, Gina, and Mark. Story told in *An Alpha's Path* and *A Night Away*.

**Kaylee Jamenson**—daughter of Josh, Reed and Hannah. Twin to Conner.

**Larissa**—deceased member of the Redwood Pack. Witch and friend to Melanie. Mate to Neil and mother of Gina and Mark.

**Lexi Jamenson**—former Talon Pack member and new Redwood Pack member. Mother to Parker and sister to Logan. Mate to North. Story told in *Hidden Destiny*.

**Logan Anderson**—former Talon Pack member and new Redwood Pack member. Uncle to Parker and brother to Lexi. Mate to Cailin. Story told in *Fighting Fate*.

**Maddox Jamenson**—Omega of the Redwood Pack. Mate to Ellie and father to Charlotte. Story told in *Shattered Emotions*.

**Mark Jamenson**—newly adopted son of Kade and Melanie. Her birth parents, Larissa and Neil were killed during an attack.

**Melanie Jamenson**—former human chemist and mate to Kade. Mother to Finn, Gina and Mark. Story told in *An Alpha's Path* and *A Night Away*.

**Meryl**—Redwood Pack Elder.

**Micah Jamenson**—son of Adam and Bay.

**Mrs. Carnoski**—elderly customer of Josh's when he was human.

**Neil**—deceased member of the Redwood Pack. Mate to Larissa and father of Gina and Mark.

**Noah**—member of the Redwood Pack and former lover of Cailin's.

**North Jamenson**—doctor in the Redwood Pack, son of the Alpha. Mate to Lexi. Story told in *Hidden Destiny*.

**Parker Jamenson**—new member of the Redwood Pack and son of Lexi's.

**Patricia (Pat) Jamenson**—mate of the Alpha, Alpha female, and mother to Kade, Jasper, Adam, Reed, Maddox, North, and Cailin.

**Patrick**—disgruntled member of The Redwood Pack.

**Reed Jamenson**—artist and son of the Alpha of the Redwood Pack. Mate to Josh and Hannah. Story told in *Trinity Bound* and *Blurred Expectations*.

**Reggie**—deceased former member of the Central Pack.

**Samuel**—deceased former member of the Central Pack.

**Willow Jamenson**—former human baker and now mate to Jasper. Mother to Brie. Story told in *A Taste for a Mate* and *A Beta's Haven*.

# CHAPTER ONE

Dying was inevitable. Being left behind was almost unbearable.

Some days she could remember the exact tone of his voice, the color of his eyes when he smiled, the way his hair looked on a breezy day.

Other days she lost all of it, the thought forgotten on the wind that carried the goddess's voice.

Emeline never thought twice about her mind and the way it worked. Not anymore. She was far too old to worry about a memory or the lack of one. She never remembered her dead mate's face. It had been too long, and honestly, she wasn't sure if she wanted to remember Jeffery any longer.

What did it matter that she was almost five hundred years old and mateless? Though she called Jeffery her mate, she knew that wasn't quite the truth. In all honesty, she'd never actually mated Jeffery. He'd left to fight a war and died before he completed the mating bond.

She's spent the entirety of her life alone, dried up, and mateless.

What a waste.

Her phone rang, bringing her out of thoughts of dead mates, old bodies, and older souls. With a sigh, she ran a hand through her shoulder-length blonde curls, knowing she must look a fright. She got up from her spot on the floor, her petite limbs cracking from sitting on the hardwood too long surrounded by books. Oh sure, she didn't have a line on her face, nor did she look like anything but the healthy twenty-something most wolves did, but she could sure feel her age. She might be a wolf that lived for hundreds of years—and had—but that didn't mean her body didn't feel it on some days.

And ever since she'd found friends within the Redwoods, she'd started to feel her age more and more.

The result of hanging with century-old and younger pups.

"Yes?" she said as she answered. She could have looked at the display on the phone, but she still wasn't used to that.

Caller ID was a new invention to her at this point.

"Oh good, I caught you. How are you, Emeline dear?"

Emeline smiled at the sound of Lexi's voice. It never failed to make her feel warm inside when the other woman spoke. No matter how much the other woman had been through, she always put a happy face and brave front on for the world. That was how she functioned and how she made it through the day. When it became too much, Lexi had her mate, North, to rely on.

Something that Emeline knew she'd never have.

Not that she'd ever truly had it to begin with. She couldn't miss what she'd never had after all.

"Hi, Lexi, how is your day going?"

"We're hanging in there." Lexi sighed, and Emeline's heart broke once again for her.

She knew why Lexi called that morning. Why she'd called every other day for the past year and a half. Her mate, North, had been blinded by the demon Caym during one of their final battles through a spell and not by a physical injury. Because of that, they all held out hope there would be a way to fix that.

Considering North was a doctor—or had been one before the accident—his livelihood was on the line. He couldn't practice medicine fully without his eyes. Yes, he was a wolf and could do other things, and even work alongside others, but it wasn't the same. As it was, the new doctor, Noah, was working out, and people liked him. That didn't mean North would be okay with that forever.

As for Noah...no...Emeline wouldn't think about him just then.

She didn't know if she even could. Not without feeling that odd pang in her heart.

As the months, days, and now years passed since North's injury, the hope for his recovery was looking less and less likely.

The hope also resided on Emeline's shoulders alone. Yes, others had helped her, but she was the one with the knowledge and, frankly, the time to spare. She was an elder, one of the oldest wolves of the Pack, and unlike those who had been part of her elder circle, unlike how she herself had been for years before that, she wanted her role to be that of a helper and not a burden.

"Talk to me," Emeline said as she stretched down to reach her toes. She'd been sitting for hours, so entrenched in her books, she hadn't noticed that half the day was already gone. Speaking of, she should probably get something to eat soon.

Day in and day out, the life of a wolf who lived alone—and would probably continue to live alone—seemed pretty boring. Even now that the war with the Centrals had been over for a year, the den for Emeline was quiet and peaceful.

But she wouldn't say boring.

Not anymore.

Not since she'd moved out of the elder's inner circle and into one of the extra Jamenson homes near the Alpha's house.

Maybe she should get a cat or something.

Oh yes, that would be great. She could become the five-hundred-year-old cat-lady werewolf. Because people didn't think she was crazy enough with the way her mind wandered and the fact that sometimes she could hear the moon goddess's voice in her head.

"Emeline? You still there?"

Crap. She'd done it again. Freaking old age was killing her attention span, and she felt more like a squirrel with a new bag of nuts.

Emeline closed her eyes and tried to think back to the bits and pieces she must have gleaned from having a half ear on the conversation, only to come up short. Apparently today was one of her bad days when it came to playing normal.

"Sorry, I let my mind wander. What was it, honey?"

"Are you taking care of yourself?" Lexi asked, concern in her tone. "You're not working too hard on your research, are you? Because...well...because no matter what happens with North, you know that we will always think of you as family. We want you to be healthy too. So don't put your whole soul into it and hurt yourself. Your wellbeing is important too."

"I'm minding myself, Lexi. Please don't worry about me. Tell me about your day and that baby of yours."

The Jamensons had found themselves in a baby boom of sorts. Each of the seven siblings that ran the Pack had recently had children. Within the last eight months, each of the Jamensons had had babies. Emeline had a feeling she knew exactly what all of them had been doing the moment they knew the war they'd fought for years was finally over.

Since the war with the Centrals had ended the year prior, seven new Jamenson babies had been born into the Redwood Pack and Emeline had a feeling everyone would be having another set in the coming years. They all loved children, Emeline as well, and though they all lived very long lives, having children hundreds of years apart never made sense to most wolves.

Emeline wouldn't know.

She'd never had a child.

Okay, she really needed to stop feeling so down on herself. It wasn't attractive. Not that she cared about being attractive, but indulging in a pity party wasn't on her agenda.

"Isabelle is doing great. She's such a happy baby. She sleeps through the night even. Something Parker never did. Though Parker might be a well-adjusted kid now, I swear it took until he was three for him to gain that temperament."

Parker was Lexi's son from before she'd met North and become a Redwood. North and the Jamensons had adopted him into the family without question. The whole family was like that. Welcoming, and always with open arms.

That, honestly, was most people.

Including Emeline herself. Before she'd found the Jamensons, or, rather, they'd found her, she'd stayed within the elder living area. Always. It had been over a hundred years since she'd left that area of the den before she'd found herself with the Jamensons. The late Alpha, Edward, and his wife, Pat, had come to her to meet her and talk with her. They'd even asked for her help in certain things, and she always gave what advice she could.

Just because she'd lived for hundreds of years didn't mean she'd actually *lived.*

"Emeline?"

She shook her head again, annoyed with herself for letting her mind wander. “That baby girl of yours sounds like she’s right where she’s supposed to be. You’ll let me visit her, right?”

She had no idea why she’d said that, but now that she had, she wanted the answer.

“Of course, Emeline. You know you don’t even have to ask. You’re family now.”

That thought warmed her, and she smiled, letting her finger trace a line on her thigh, trying to keep her mind on the conversation at hand rather than allowing it wander. Again.

“Well...” She stopped and licked her lips. “Thank you, Lexi. Maybe I’ll stop by tomorrow.”

“Do it. Come for dinner. Please, Emeline. You need the break, and we’d love to have you.”

“Okay. I can do that.”

So odd. She'd never really done anything as simple as a dinner with friends in so long that she wasn't even sure what she should do.

"Then we will see you there, Emeline."

"Should I bring something?"

"Just yourself unless you want to make something. It's up to you. We're informal here."

"I can bring dessert." She loved baking but hadn't done too much of it recently since, for years, it hadn't been the best idea to bake only for herself.

Now, though, she had people to bake for.

"That sounds like a plan." Lexi let out a sigh, and Emeline knew what was coming. It was always the same, and it pained her not to be able to have a good answer for the other woman. "How's research going?"

Every time Lexi asked, Emeline pictured North holding his child, unable to see her. The hollowness within her paled in comparison to what he'd lost.

"I don't have any answers for you yet. I'm sorry, Lexi. I'm trying, but I don't see it yet. I'm not giving up though."

Lexi's silence was expected, but it still didn't make Emeline feel any better. "Thank you. I know you must tire of me calling, but...but I need to. You know? I know you'd come and find us the moment you figured something out, but I feel like I need to call you. Just in case. If I ever annoy you, or hurt you because I call, tell me. I'll stop."

"You're welcome to call. In fact, I look forward to it." Well, that was depressing. Looking forward to a call from a woman who was breaking inside because she couldn't help her mate. All because Emeline needed contact with the outside world.

"If you say so." Lexi took a deep breath, audible through the phone. "Okay then. I will see you tomorrow for dinner. I can't wait to taste what you make for dessert, and I'll be sure Parker and North know you're coming as well. Thank you, Emeline. Thank you for everything."

She let the other woman go then stared at the phone, her mind on countless other things again rather than what was in front of her.

"Have you eaten yet, Em?"

Emeline screamed and jumped off the chair, phone crashing to the floor, claws bared.

"Noah?" She blinked, her chest heaving. "What are you doing in my home? How did you get in here? And why are you here scaring the life out of me?"

He smiled at her, and Emeline wanted to strangle him.

This man. This *wolf*.

He just wouldn't leave her alone.

The pup was twenty-eight for God's sake. A mere blip in the radar of her long life. It didn't matter that her wolf practically preened when he smiled. No, she didn't want any of that.

That stupid dimple on his cheek deepened, and Emeline held back a growl. She refused to notice the long, lean lines of his body, the waves of chestnut hair that fell to the back of his neck, or the muscles that bulged just right when he bent to pick something up.

Nope.

She didn't want this pup.

No matter what her wolf said.

# CHAPTER TWO

Noah smiled at the wide-eyed look on Emeline's face. Considering he came to her place at least three times a week, she shouldn't have been surprised that he was there. However, he didn't think she really understood *why* he was there, so maybe he could forgive her for her being startled.

At least a little.

Her blond curls lay in a tangle on her shoulders, as if she'd been running her hand through them throughout the day while she was buried in texts. Those violet eyes held a wealth of knowledge and an innocence he didn't quite understand.

Or maybe he did and he wasn't sure what to do with it.

At least not yet.

She stood at least a foot shorter than him, all pixie and gentle, until someone pissed her off; then she was all wolf, biting, clawing, and forcing her way to independence

The perfect woman for him.

If only she felt the same way.

"Well, Noah? What are you doing here?"

Was it wrong to love the little line that formed between her brows when she got angry with him? He had issues, apparently.

With a small smile, ignoring the fact she didn't seem pleased to see him, he brought his hand out from behind his back, the clutch of wildflowers he held looking slightly wilted on the edges. His nerves were starting to grate on him.

Her eyes brightened for a moment—making his wolf howl—before she narrowed them in suspicion.

"Why are you bringing me flowers, Noah?"

Noah raised his brows then shrugged before moving past her to the kitchen. He knew where she kept her vases in this new place and took care of getting the flowers in water for her. He could feel her presence behind him, that calm, yet unearthly quality that he was falling for as each day passed.

It took everything within him not to fall completely.

She might be his mate, the other half of his soul, but from the way she acted around him, he didn't think she felt the same way.

The sharp pang across his heart was as subtle as a dull blade, but he ignored it. He might be only twenty-eight to her five hundred, but he had all the patience in the world.

He had to, considering fate had given him a sheltered elder for a mate.

"Noah? You can't just come in here and start taking over."

He placed the vase on the breakfast island counter then turned to face Emeline. "I wanted to bring you flowers, Em. You can at least say thank you."

She shut her eyes, her chest lifting as she took a deep breath. She opened her eyes again and the lost look that was always there broke him just that much more. “I’m sorry. Thank you for the flowers. They’re beautiful.” Her gaze drifted to the wilting wildflowers, and Noah held back a wince.

She probably had received dozens of flowers from her late mate and countless others in her lifetime. Beautiful buds that made his dingy sprouts pale in comparison. He hadn’t thought to bring her any when he’d set out to her place that afternoon. No, he’d seen them on the hillside and thought of her smile.

He didn’t tell her any of that though. As it was, he was sure he scared her enough with just his presence. He still wasn’t sure how to fix that, but he’d find a way.

As he studied her face, wanting to memorize every contour for when she sent him on his away again, he saw what he’d missed before. The dark shadows under her eyes had grown more pronounced since the last time he'd seen her, as had the paleness of her face.

He knew that working on a cure for North's blindness was taking a toll on her, but right then, she looked even worse. It didn't help matters that she'd about killed herself when they'd sent the demon Caym, who had almost killed them all, back to hell.

She'd saved them all with her insight, wisdom, and countless hours spent with her nose in a book.

And she'd sacrificed her health in the process.

He'd spent the past year trying to get her to *see* him while not scaring her away. At the same time, he'd slowly worked on getting her back to a healthy weight and schedule of sleeping and eating.

By the look of her right then, his efforts hadn't been good enough.

"Have you eaten today, Em?"

She narrowed her eyes again. "Why do you keep calling me Em? My name is Emeline. Use it."

He tucked a piece of hair behind her ear, and the stillness of her body at his touch set his wolf on edge, but he let it pass. He'd get her used to him.

"I like calling you Em. Everyone else calls you Emeline, so I wanted to use something different."

"That makes no sense, Noah. I'm nothing to you. I'm just an elder."

The words sliced through him, and he had to hold back everything he'd wanted to say to her since he first laid eyes on her in the Alpha's home. She was his mate. A potential. His wolf had known from the first scent and the man had known from the first look. There were only a few—if not just the one—potentials in the world throughout a wolf's lifetime that could become a mate. If both parties fell for one another, they'd form a mating bond, connect their souls, and start their journey into their long lives together.

Noah had never heard of someone finding their potential mate, only to realize that the other felt nothing.

Fate wasn't that cruel.

However, maybe because Emeline was an elder, she was different. Noah knew she had a connection to the moon goddess, their deity that had created wolves in the first place long ago, and had more memories than he could ever dream of, so maybe that meant her wolf worked in a way he'd yet to understand.

Just because he didn't think she recognized him as a mate didn't mean he'd give up. No, he'd take it one day at a time. Court her until she saw in him what he saw in her.

Until then, he needed to keep her healthy.

After all, since North was incapacitated until they found a way to heal him, Noah was the Pack doctor—something he never thought he'd truly be doing on his own at this young an age.

Best not think of him as young when Emeline was already thinking of him as a pup. While others might frown on the age difference, he didn't care. They were wolves. It wasn't as though he was a teenager, and it wasn't as though she actually looked her age.

No, they both looked to be in their twenties, and though she had more practical experience, he wasn't about to be left behind.

He shook his head then cupped her face. She didn't pull away this time. Progress.

"Did you eat, Em?" At her sigh, he rubbed her cheekbone with his thumb. "Don't change the subject like you normally do. You need to take care of yourself."

She rolled her eyes then pulled away. He didn't frown at the loss because at least she'd stayed in his hold for as long as she had. It could have been worse. She could have looked revolted and run away at the first hint of a caress.

It was the little things—like her momentary acceptance—that made courting worth it.

"No, I haven't eaten yet. I got caught up in spells then Lexi called, and I got distracted again."

Noah let out a breath then went to her fridge to get out the salad fixings he'd put in there two days before.

"Noah, I can take care of myself. Stop acting like a dominant ass."

He raised a brow then took out a hunk of goat cheese and some apricot and herbed jam he'd bought as well. "I know you can. You're just spending way too much time worrying about others. It's okay. North needs us. But now I'm going to make sure you're cared for as well." He made her a small plate of goat cheese, jam, and thick croutons he'd made at home for her. The croutons were really more like small bread slices that went well with the softness of the goat cheese.

"Eat, Em. I'll make you a salad. You'll need protein though. Do you still have that salmon?"

She rolled her eyes then took a bite of the bread and cheese. A small amount of the creamy filling dotted her lip, and her tongue slid across the curve, cleaning her mouth in the sexiest movement he'd ever seen her make.

Not that she'd done it to be sexy.

But hell.

"It's in the middle drawer where it wouldn't spoil right away," she answered then put her hand on his back. He froze, relishing her touch. She didn't open touch him purposely, no, in fact, it was only when she was bleeding, out of breath, or passing out that she reached out to him. This though, this wasn't any of those.

His wolf loved it.

"Do you need anything to drink?" he asked, his voice oddly thick. Great, he was acting the age she'd always treated him, not the man who'd been through war and had started to fall in love with the woman behind him.

"Thank you, Noah. I know I'm being stupid by not accepting your help. You do so much for me, and yet I push you away. I just hate that my mind wanders so much that I forget to take care of myself. I'm getting so old and senile it's a wonder that I'm not put out to pasture."

His wolf snarled. He set the salmon and milk jug on the counter and turned, cupping her face. She let out a little gasp, but he ignored it because he needed to get the words out.

"You are not senile. Your mind works more than any other wolf I know. You're working your butt off for others, Em. So what if you forget to eat? People younger than you tend to forget what they're supposed to be doing for themselves when they're focused on other things. It makes you scatterbrained. Not old. Get the thought out of your head that you need to be, as you put it, put out to pasture, or anything like that. You got me? You don't get to talk about yourself like that in my presence. You saved us all, Em. You did it with your mind, your heart, and your strength. You're allowed to forget a meal or two."

She swallowed hard, and it took all within him not to bend and brush his lips against hers. She wasn't ready for that. And come to think of it, he wasn't sure if he was either. Because once he did, he wouldn't be able to stop.

"You get me, Em?"

"I get you."

"Good." He cleared his throat then let her go. "You want your salmon grilled or baked?"

"I can help you," she said, her voice soft. "I'm not an invalid."

"Never said you were. And since you've got enough salmon for two, can I join you?"

She raised a brow. "You usually eat with me most days you stop by anyway and you've never asked before. You just do it."

He gave her a sheepish grin. "I'm trying not to act like a dominant ass."

She blushed and ducked her head before taking out the portable grill for the salmon. "I didn't mean it when I said that before. I'm just a little out of sorts and seem to be taking it out on you."

He took out the cutting board and started slicing avocados, orange peppers, and grape tomatoes to go on the top of their salads. If he'd been thinking, he'd have boiled a couple eggs for more protein before heading over, but it was too late now.

"You're welcome to take anything you want out on me." Did that sound dirty? Because it sure did to him. He'd have to watch himself.

"I don't know how to repay you, Noah. What you did on the field against Caym..." She took a deep breath, and it took all in Noah's power not to stop what he was doing and hold her. "You saved me. You tell me that I saved the Pack, but without you holding me up, keeping me going, I wouldn't have made it. The magic I had to use...well...it hurt." She gave him a small smile at the lie she'd just told.

Oh yeah, he knew it was a lie. The magic she'd used to send the demon to hell had more than hurt. If they'd been mated at the time, he was pretty sure he could have helped her even more through the bond, but that was neither here nor there. Now he had a woman healing and learning to be part of a Pack again while he was learning to be a greater part of a Pack. They would be great together.

If only she could see it.

"Go out with me, Em."

She froze, her eyes wide. The salmon popped on the grill beside her, but neither of them moved to take care of it.

"Out? Like out out?"

For someone who'd lived centuries, she sure didn't understand everything she thought she did. No worries, though, he'd teach her. He'd show her everything.

He set down the knife, turned down the grill behind her—the action forcing her to move closer to him—then quirked his lips.

"Yes, out out. You and me. On a date."

"But why?"

He tried not to wince at that but failed miserably. He could have said he wanted to go out with her because they were mates and fated to be together. That once they did, once they mated, they would each be destined for a future filled with bliss, babies, and lots of time panting.

Considering he wasn't even sure she could *feel* her wolf wanting him that way, he had a feeling he should keep those thoughts to himself.

"Why?"

"No, no, that's not what I meant. Oh, Noah, I'm sure a nice young wolf would go out with you. You don't have to pity date the old woman who lives alone."

Okay, now he was getting angry. "Don't patronize me, Em. I asked *you* out. You. No one else. I want to take you out on a date. You're not an old woman who doesn't deserve to be cherished.

You're Emeline. An Elder and a fucking amazing woman. So please, come out with me."

She blinked again. "Well then. If you're so passionate about it. You know I haven't been on a date in...well...let's not talk about that."

He grinned at her and brushed her hair behind her ear. "Sounds like a plan to me."

She might not know what she was feeling, but once she knew the world was waiting for her, she'd see. He knew it. He'd just have to hunt her heart like a mate on the prowl.

# CHAPTER THREE

"I'm a cougar. A cougar on the prowl."

Lexi and Bay Jamenson cracked up laughing, almost falling off the bed they were sitting on surrounded by piles of discarded dresses and pants, but Emeline didn't find it funny. Oh no. Not at all.

The two of them were her friends. An odd thing to say after

so many years of staying within the elder community of eight or so wolves who had grown bored of each other ages ago. Now Bay and Lexi were there to help her dress for her date with Noah.

Her date.

With Noah.

Goddess, what had she been thinking?

"I'm a cougar, ladies. Isn't that what it's called? Some past-her-prime woman who chases after young men so she can have her way with them before tossing them away for a younger version? They want all that virility and energy, and want to remember what it's like to be youthful. A cougar. I'm a cougar."

"Oh, honey, please stop calling yourself a cougar," Lexi said, tears streaming from her eyes.

Emeline put her fists on her hips and scowled. "That's what I am, aren't I?"

"No, Emeline, you're a wolf," Bay said, clearly trying not to smile and failing badly. "A female wolf about to go on a date with a very sexy male wolf. Stop calling yourself a cougar. Though, oh my god, that's hilarious."

Good for them to think she was funny. Emeline felt nothing of the sort. Well, maybe on the verge of being a joke, but she was sure she was going crazy.

Thank the goddess Bay and Lexi were there. Though Emeline was friends with all of the Jamensons, these two were closer to her than the others. Even closer than Reed. Reed, the artist of the family, had known her for the longest—other than his late parents of course. He had worked with her for years on persevering the Pack's history in art form.

He'd always treated her with reverence and extreme care, and that same reverence made it hard now for them to become as close as she was with Bay and Lexi.

She'd met Bay when the woman had found her locket, the locket Emeline had put in her jewelry case that morning knowing she wouldn't be wearing it for the evening. Maybe not ever again. Jeffery had given it to her before he'd set off for war against a rival Pack, only to never come home to see her wear it. She'd thrown it into the fire when she found out Jeffery had died, her pain too much to bear. She and Bay had bonded over the shared memories and pain, becoming close ever since.

Lexi, of course, had become close to Emeline during the trials and research concerning North. Right then, though, none of that was on the table.

No, today was all about Emeline and Noah.

And their date.

"What am I supposed to do on a date with a wolf Cailin used to date?" She ran her hand through her hair, annoyed she'd even said that last part. She loved Cailin Jamenson Anderson. The lone daughter of the set of Jamensons she felt connected to, Cailin had been by her side in the final battle. That didn't mean she necessarily wanted to think about her or any other woman with Noah.

Not that Emeline had any reason to be jealous.

She didn't even want Noah.

*Sure, keep telling yourself that.*

"He's more than Cailin's ex, Emeline," Bay said softly.

"Darn it. Don't you think I know that? He's a doctor. He saves people. He puts everyone before himself, and now I'm sure he's stressed himself out enough that he's asking me out on a pity date. That's got to be it. He's so exhausted from working at the clinic that he's delirious."

Lexi stood up and raised her brows. "Stop doing this to yourself. He's a nice wolf who wants to date you. He's taking you out for a hike and a picnic. It's sweet. He's not doing this out of pity. He's doing this because he wants you."

Emeline closed her eyes then pulled her shirt over her head before stomping to the closet. She pulled another one on, this one a nice tan cotton top that looked nice and would be good for a hike.

This was the fifth shirt she'd tried, and she'd been through four pairs of pants. She was over-thinking it. She knew that, but she couldn't help herself. It was just a date. An outing with a younger man.

Crap.

"Why would he want me? He needs to be out looking for his mate, not wasting his time with a dried-up elder."

Bay and Lexi gave each other a look that Emeline couldn't decipher. That wasn't uncommon though, considering Emeline had isolated herself for so long. She always seemed to be missing something or another.

"What?" she asked at their look.

Bay shook her head then kissed Emeline on the cheek before moving so Lexi could do the same. "You're going to be fine, honey. Enjoy tonight and stop worrying about the what-ifs and everything else in that head of yours. That wolf on his way wants to enjoy the evening with you. Let it happen. You said yes, so enjoy the fact that you did. Okay?"

Slightly numb, Emeline nodded.

"Now we will get out of your hair since you look like you're ready to go. Plus we don't want to be in the house when Noah gets here. This way it's all about you."

Again, Emeline nodded before saying goodbye to her friends. That left her alone in her house with too many thoughts and worries. Just like the ones the girls had told her to forget.

Darn it.

Her wolf scented him before he knocked on the door.

That scent of forest and wolf that somehow calmed her own wolf. Emeline hadn't been able to make sense of it considering nothing had done that for her wolf in years...if ever. She couldn't exactly remember.

She opened the door and held back a gasp at her first sight of him. His tousled brown waves framed his face, brushing the collar of his shirt, making him look rugged and handsome. His blue eyes held laughter and a touch of something she couldn't quite name, something unique she now associated with Noah.

The hiking clothes he wore formed to his body, making his already strong, toned muscles look even more dangerous.

From the way her wolf batted at her, she had a feeling her wolf *liked* this sense of danger.

Steeling herself with a deep breath, she smiled. "Noah."

"Em," he growled softly. See? There was that danger again. "You look amazing."

She raised a brow, even as she relaxed inside at his compliment. "I'm good for hiking, right?"

He grinned then, that dimple deepening. That damn dimple. "You're good for anything, Em. Just saying. Now let's head to the spot I picked out." He stepped back and allowed her to move forward, shutting the door behind her. When he held his hand out, she hesitated only a moment before putting her small hand in his much larger one.

The warmth of his palm sent sizzles down her arm, and the calluses on his fingertips sent zings to other parts of her body.

Apparently she hadn't been taking care of her need for touch if a simple handhold was about to send her over the edge.

She smiled, trying to put those thoughts away before she went crazy and jumped him. Nope, this was just a casual date. No jumping or moaning allowed.

*Oh goddess, who said anything about moaning?*

"You okay, Em? You look flushed."

She blinked then shook her head. "I'm fine. Really. Uh, must be the air." Oh good, because that wasn't the most idiotic thing she could have said. It was as if she hadn't been on a date in a century or two.

Okay, so she hadn't been on a date in a century or two.

Whatever.

Noah squeezed her hand and started moving toward the tree line at the edge of the Jamenson property within the den.

"You don't need to be nervous, Em. It's just a meal and a hike. Nothing too scary."

"You would be nervous too if this was your first date in over a century," she blurted out then immediately wanted to take her words back. Noah didn't need to know that. She already thought he felt sorry for her. That would just be icing on the cake of pity and shame.

"A century, huh?" Noah jumped over a fallen log, releasing her hand in the process. As he turned back to help her over, she raised a brow then leaped over it herself. She was a werewolf after all. Chivalry might be nice, but she wasn't about to show her belly to a dominant wolf when she was dominant as well. Maybe not as dominant as him, but enough that she just needed to remind them both that she was a predator capable of defending herself.

It was so odd to think about that since she'd locked herself away for so long. Dominance games and courting were so far out of her recent experience she felt as though she was floundering, but from the laugh that escaped Noah at her act, maybe she wasn't as rusty as she'd thought.

"Touché, Em. You're a strong wolf. I've never forgotten that. I was just trying to help."

"I know. For some reason my wolf needed to show you she was there too."

He brought her hand to his lips, gently brushing a kiss against her skin. Again she wanted to moan or rub up along his side, cover him with her scent so everyone would know he was hers and hers alone.

She pulled back, stunned at her own thoughts.

What on earth had that been about?

"I know. I've always known." He cleared his throat then pulled her along the trail toward wherever he had set up their lunch. "Okay, so back to the century thing. How have you not been on a date in that long?

You're gorgeous, funny, and loyal as hell. What the hell is wrong with our Pack that you haven't dated in that long?"

She almost tripped over a stray root at his words but kept going. "You really think all that."

He stopped them both, turned, then cupped her face. She sucked in a breath at the warmth of his skin and the look in his eyes.

"Of course I do. I'm here aren't I? Em..." He trailed off then sighed. "You keep selling yourself short, and I think that's because you've cut yourself off for so long. You're an elder so you think you have to act staid and remain alone. That's not the case. All of the elders could have moved into the other areas of the den and blended. We all age the same way and look to be in our twenties or thirties. Our bodies only ache from fighting or being too lazy to get off the couch. You're thriving now that you've left the elder area. Why didn't you do that before?"

"That's a lot to take in, Noah. We stay in the elder area because that's how it's done. Or at least, that's how it's been done in the past."

"But you moved out."

She smiled then, and he ran his thumbs along her cheekbones as he pulled back. "Yes. I moved out. *I* didn't want to be shut in anymore. Researching and finding a way to send Caym back to hell after all those years took a toll on me. Not only physically but mentally and emotionally as well. I wasn't the same person after everything that happened."

"I don't think any of us are."

"We've all changed, and despite what Meryl—she's one of the lead elders if you can call her that—wants, some of the elders are starting to move on and spread out."

"So it's this Meryl who didn't want you to move away?"

She almost said no, then thought about it. Meryl had been the one who told her to stay for as long as she had. And since Emeline had no other family, it had been the easiest decision.

"I suppose so. But it doesn't matter now. I'm out of that area and trying to be the wolf I used to be. Or at least a wolf that I can be proud of."

"You should be proud of yourself no matter what, Em."

"Thanks for that." She turned toward the trail, gesturing in that direction. "Should we keep going?"

"Sounds like a plan to me." He took her hand again, this time tangling their fingers. Her wolf gave a happy sigh and she had to refrain from doing the same aloud. "As for dating? Are you going to answer that?"

How to answer that...

"Well, since I never left the elder area, there really wasn't much to choose from."

Noah's neck pinked, and she blushed as well. "So, uh, it's been a hundred years since you've..."

Emeline froze then faced him. "Uh...no...There was a man named Edgar." She closed her eyes, wondering how on earth she'd ended up in this conversation. "We didn't date per se, it was more of... scratching the itch. We're wolves after all. We need touch."

Noah gave a strangled growl, his eyes shut tight. "I shouldn't have asked that. It was rude and honestly...damn it. I shouldn't have asked that."

She grinned at him, liking that he was all flustered. Now he knew how she felt constantly around him. Which was why, after she asked the next question, she wanted to fling herself off the nearest bridge.

"I take it Cailin was the last person you were with?"

Dear. Goddess.

Why had she asked that?

Noah's eyes widened, and he blushed just as hard as she probably was. "Yes. So it's been awhile. And Cailin and I are just friends. We used to be close, but she's my best friend now. I'm close to Logan too. Her mate. Is that okay?"

"Why wouldn't it be? I mean you're not with her now obviously. She's mated. And you're here with me."

She liked that. Him here with her. No matter how nervous she'd been at the start, she liked her hand in his, his wolf near hers. She could get used to it.

That was the exact reason she needed to be cautious. He could find his mate at any moment. It wouldn't be good to get her hopes up when they would crash down at the first sign of fate's interference.

"Okay then. So it's good that I do this."

He cupped her face, and she froze for a moment. Then as his lips brushed hers, she closed her eyes, sinking into him. The slight touch of his tongue against her lips made her moan, and she parted her lips for him. He took that as an invitation—and rightly so. She moved her hands up his back, pulling him closer as he deepened this kiss.

Her wolf howled, begging for more, and she could feel his wolf also, pushing, prodding, demanding.

Oh, how she wanted it all.

Craved it all.

Then he pulled back, breathless, his eyes dark yet rimmed with gold.

Aroused then.

Well, so was she.

Oh goddess, so was she.

"Let's do that again," she breathed.

He smiled full-out, white teeth against tan skin. "Let's. But, first, let me take you to the picnic area. We're almost there." He took her hand, and they started on their way. "And, Em?"

"Yes, Noah?"

"This is one hell of a first date."

She licked her lips, his taste still on her tongue. "Oh yes. Definitely."

And she couldn't wait for the second one.

# CHAPTER FOUR

Noah needed help.

Badly.

He stood outside North's door, but didn't knock. Sure, those inside could probably scent him, but he needed to calm himself and clear his thoughts before he walked in there and asked for help.

He'd never truly courted a woman before, and he had a

feeling he was going about it all wrong. Shouldn't Emeline know by now if he was a potential mate for her? He could feel the connection, feel the pull of his wolf, the swift shock of desire every time he laid eyes on her.

Hell, he could feel it at just the thought of her small smile and violet eyes.

Yet she showed no signs of feeling the same way.

No, in fact, she was *surprised* he wanted to be with her, rather than some young female wolf that would mean nothing to him. Everyone who might fit that bill paled in comparison to Emeline.

As if he'd be with anyone else.

Still, what if fate got it wrong? Maybe what he had was a strong case of lust and attraction.

His wolf raged within, scraping his claws along the inside of Noah's chest, and he winced.

Okay, so that had been an idiotic idea.

Emeline was his.

He just had to prove it.

He had a feeling she couldn't tell they were mates because it had been so long since she'd ever felt anything like it. Like it or not, she'd had a mate, Jeffrey, in the past and Noah would have to get over that.

She'd been oddly okay with his past with Cailin, and that was even more recent.

Though the fact she was readily okay with it wasn't a good sign in itself. Maybe she didn't think he was worth the trouble to get even a little jealous over.

Damn it. He needed to stop thinking about the worst-case scenarios—as in fate had fucked him over and chosen a mate who wanted nothing to do with him in any way possible—and find a way into Emeline's heart.

It would happen.

He was sure of it.

It would just be slow going.

He was okay with that though. All of the best things were worth the time it took to gain them.

With that thought, he finally knocked on the door.

Logan answered the door, his brows raised. "Took you long enough to knock."

Noah grinned then walked inside, being sure to ram his shoulder into Logan's as he did. Just because he had only friendly feelings for Logan's mate now, it was still fun to badger the wolf. Logan snorted then pushed at him.

Hard.

Noah barely kept his balance and made his way to the couch where North sat drinking a beer. The other man faced him though Noah knew North couldn't see him. Damn it, he and Emeline would fix this. No matter what. The man deserved to see his daughter and live his life to the fullest.

North might have been making due, but he was still a dominant wolf who'd lost his sight.

There was no coming back from that.

Not fully.

"Stop staring at me and feeling bad, Noah. I'm fine. Emeline is working on it, and I'm getting by. It's not the end of the world. Now grab a beer and tell us your troubles."

Logan snorted then took a seat in the armchair across from them. "Yes, tell us about your love life. I'm sure we can help. Since, you know, we're connected to our feelings and all that shit."

Noah grinned then took a sip of the beer they'd put on the table for him. The bitter, hearty brew was just what he needed to soothe his throat and calm his nerves enough to even ask for help in the first place.

"You're happily mated, and I know for a fact that you get romantic with Cailin, so don't start on that feeling shit." Noah grinned as Logan frowned. Goddess, he loved making fun of Logan. He couldn't help it. The other wolf was more dominant, alpha as hell, and a good man.

"How much does Cailin tell you? I'm going to have to spank that ass of hers if she doesn't keep things private."

Noah choked on his beer, and North slammed his hand on his back a couple times.

"For the love of god, Logan. Don't talk about spanking my sister's ass. Ever. Jesus."

Logan grinned, unrepentant, then winced as if he'd just

remembered North couldn't see that grin. Shit, they needed to help North.

"Stop frowning," North snapped. "I knew you were acting like an ass. Just because I can't see doesn't mean I don't know. Anyway, Noah, what have you done to court our dear Emeline? We want her happy, you know. And since she's an honorary Jamenson, we'll kick your ass if you hurt her."

Noah relaxed immediately. Yes, these two would help as much as they could. "First, tell her that. Not the ass-kicking part. But the Jamenson part. I think she needs to feel like she's truly part of a family and not just on the fringes."

North nodded. "We're trying. She's surrounded by a hard shell that's tough to crack. But we're Jamensons. We don't back down from a challenge."

"Good. As for hurting her? That's not on my radar, man. She's my mate. I just don't think she knows it yet."

Logan shook his head. "The thing is, I agree with you. As much as it pains me. But the way she's let you help her this past year? That means something. She's one strong wolf, and the fact that she leans on you tells me her wolf is ready for you. I just don't think the human is connecting the way she should."

Noah's mouth ran dry despite the beer. "You mean like with Lexi being latent or the fact that she doesn't want me at all?"

Logan held up a hand. "This is nothing like what happened with my sister."

North patted Noah's knee. "My mate felt me as her own even though she couldn't feel her own wolf. So, yeah, this is different than with Lexi. I think what

Logan is trying to say is that Emeline has spent so long on a different level than the rest of us she might not be aware that what she's feeling is mating urge."

"And I can't come out and tell her what she's feeling," Noah said drily.

Both men snorted. "Uh no. Do that and you'll have your balls sent to you in a little bag," Logan said.

"Yeah, never tell a woman what she feels. You're asking for a beat down."

"There's no easy answer to this," Logan said, his voice serious. "All you can do is do what you're doing. Show her she's the one for you. Court her. Flowers, chocolate, sweet things she might like that only you would know about. Help her with her research, make yourself such a part of her daily life that you're needed."

"So keep doing what I'm already doing then," Noah said. "There's no magic answer to this, is there?"

North sighed. "Magic can't fix everything. Also, I would wait to tell her about your mating. Knowing Emeline, she'll run because she doesn't feel it. I know that's keeping a secret, and if Lexi heard me saying this, she'd kick my ass, but I think it's for the best."

Noah nodded. "That's why I haven't told her. Plus, to be honest, I'm scared to death that I'm setting myself up for a fall and she *knows* we aren't mates. How fucked up would that be?"

"I mated a woman who was already mated to a sick son of a bitch, Noah," North whispered. "I know how fucked-up fate can be. But we made it work. You can too. Now go court your lady and make her happy. And remember what we said. Hurt her, we hurt you."

"Understood." Noah stood, said goodbye then headed to Willow's Bakery.

The Beta's mate had opened her bakery soon after she'd mated Jasper, and it was one of his favorite places to go. He figured he'd get Emeline something sweet to eat while she was studying. And if he had his way, he'd be right by her side helping. He'd already had a full day at the clinic, and thankfully, since they weren't at war, he hadn't been too slammed. Plus the Pack had a Healer, Hannah, who worked with her powers to Heal those in need. Together, he and Hannah had the Pack covered. Hopefully soon, North would be back, and they would become Noah's dream team.

One day at a time though.

"I see you made it out in one piece."

Noah rolled his eyes at Cailin's words then held out his arms. Cailin raised a brow and handed her son, Edward, over. The little guy's eyes brightened, and he waved his arms. Noah stuck his nose along the boy's neck, inhaling that sweet baby scent. He'd helped deliver every single one of the Jamenson children who had been born that year, but Edward held a special place in his heart.

Probably because of who his parents were...and who the little boy was named after. That, though, wasn't something he wanted to think about. Not when he had this little pudgy kid in his arms who smiled as if there wasn't anything wrong in the world.

Oh, to be that innocent.

"You look good with a baby in your arms," Cailin said with a smile. Her green eyes glittered, and Noah snorted.

"One thing at a time, Cai." He bounced Edward in his arms, loving the high-pitched squeals the little boy made.

Cailin winced but didn't say anything. After all, Noah was Edward's godfather and one of his favorite people. What could she say to him?

"So, are you here for a certain wolf?"

Noah rolled his eyes then went to the display case. Willow's baked goods were seriously amazing, and he could never decide on one thing. Knowing him, he'd get one of each, a cookie or two, three brownies, some cinnamon rolls, and box them up. Actually, that sounded like a plan to him.

Cailin came up to his side, leaning on his shoulder as she held her hand out to Edward. Noah shifted so the baby could grip his mother's hand, his attention on the cookies and not what was going on around him.

When Emeline's scent reached his nose, he knew he was in trouble. The fear, anger…disappointment radiating off of her threw him for a loop. He turned, Edward in hand, and Cailin at his side.

Well shit.

"I was just coming in for something to eat," Emeline said softly then tilted her head. "I don't think I'm hungry anymore." Her brows bunched, confusion clear on her face, and then she shot out of the building.

"Go get your mate, Noah. Her emotions are running all over the place with the mating urge riding her so she's not thinking clearly."

"You know she's feeling the mating urge?" he asked quickly even as he handed Edward over, ready to bolt after Emeline.

"Of course. She might not know what it is, but it's there. Now leave." She winked. "Then tell me what happens."

He nodded, kissed Edward goodbye, and then ran out of the building on Emeline's trail. She hadn't gone far, but she'd moved faster than he thought she would. Crap. This was not going according to plans.

When her scent increased, he picked up the pace and let out a breath when he spotted her sitting on a fallen log on the way to her home.

"Em."

"I don't know what's wrong with me," she said, not facing him. "I *know* she's mated to Logan. I mean, for goddess's sake, you were holding her *child*.

It wasn't as if you were with her in any sense other than being her friend. I honestly have no idea why I acted like that, and I don't like that I did. I think I was...jealous." She said the word as though she'd eaten something bad, and she grimaced. "I'm not some jealous groupie, Noah. I don't like acting like that."

He cautiously sat next to her then wrapped his arm around her shoulders. She leaned into him, letting out a breath.

"Your wolf went a little territorial, and you didn't know what to do with it. That's fine."

"But...I'm not yours...not fully...right?"

He closed his eyes, the pain hitting him hard, like blades against flesh. "Em, we're dating." A small word for it, but she would get there. Goddess, he hoped she'd get there. "You're allowed to want me to be faithful. We're exclusive. It's you and me. No one else. So if you walk into a room, and you feel like there needs to be a ten-foot space around me and other women, I'm not going to freak out. We're wolves. Sometimes we need to stake our claim." He wished it was a mating claim, but that would be another day. "You trust me, and I trust you. That's all we need to know."

"I feel like an idiot for running like that."

He turned her in his arms and brushed her cheek. "You're not an idiot. You're just having an off day. We all have them."

*Have me. Mate me. Find that connection.*

Of course, he didn't say any of that. He just prayed he wasn't shooting himself in the foot for wanting to wait for her to find it on her own and not force it.

Damn it. Waiting was hard.

When she looked up at him, those violet eyes filled with the same yearning he felt deep down in his soul, he gave in and pressed his lips to hers. She moaned beneath him, flicking her tongue along his lips. He groaned, deepening the kiss, but not pushing it further than that. As much as he wanted to throw them both to the ground and sink his cock into her pussy, grip her hips, and ride her until they were both spent, he knew this wasn't the time.

He pulled back, breathless.

"I was going in there to get you something to snack on while we researched for North," she whispered after a moment.

Noah grinned. "I was there for the same reason. What do you say we go and get a box of cookies then head to my place? We can look over texts and try to help North. Together."

She smiled then. “That sounds perfect.”

If only she’d find him perfect for her. One day at a time. It might kill him, but he’d wait for her.

Forever.

# CHAPTER FIVE

Emeline's paws hit the ground at a run, the wind brushing through her fur. She inhaled the crisp scent of nature, forest, and Pack, letting it sink deep into her soul. While it wasn't the full moon and, therefore, not a full moon hunt, Emeline had wanted to run as a wolf. All wolves could shift no matter the phase of the moon, and the stronger the wolf, the more times they could change in a given day.

She wasn't the strongest of wolves by far, but she was in no way weak. Since she'd made an idiot of herself in the bakery the day before, she'd been on edge. Other than having sex, she couldn't think of another way to settle her nerves. Before she'd left the elders, she'd probably have gone to Edgar's to, as she'd told Noah, scratch that itch; she wouldn't be doing that again. No, in fact, just the thought of being with anyone other than Noah made her want to shudder.

Thinking of Noah between her thighs, his thick cock sinking deep inside her, however, led her to a new form of shuddering altogether.

Her paw caught a root, and she rolled forward. Thankfully, she made it to her feet again without slamming her head into the ground, but hell, that had been close. She needed to keep her mind off Noah's cock and on what was going on around her.

She put Noah and whatever the hell was going on with her brain to the side and finished her run, letting her wolf take over. By the time she'd shifted back, showered, and dressed, she was running late for her date with Noah.

Well, it was almost a date. More like food while researching at his place. They were close to helping North. Emeline knew it. And having Noah there helped because he looked into the medical aspects of each magical curse and charm. He also hindered her thinking because she couldn't stop wanting to rub her whole body over him. Goddess, she wanted him.

Not that she could have him forever. Despite what her body wanted and how happy her wolf was when he was near, she wasn't his mate.

After all, she would know if that were the case. Right?

She shook her head and put those thoughts away again. No good would come from them. Yes, others had made marriages and babies with other wolves without a mating bond. With the chance of finding one's mate such a slim thing over time, sometimes wolves just made a relationship work without that extra bond with their partner. While Emeline had started to think she could do that with Noah, she knew she couldn't see him go through life without the mating bond. She cared for him too much to keep him from everything he deserved.

That thought, above all else, just about killed her.

By the time she made it to Noah's her wolf was on edge again and her heart lay heavy. She wasn't sure how much longer she could stand to be with him knowing she'd have to give him up. Decisions would have to be made soon, but not now. No, first they needed to help North. Then she could help herself.

Noah opened the door before she could knock, that dimple in his cheek deepening as he smiled. "Em, you're here." He ran a hand through her wet hair and pulled her close. "And all sparkly clean. Mmmm." He kissed her hard then let go, leaving her aching.

"Hello, Noah," she finally said.

"I made finger foods and antipasto so it will be easy for us to nibble while we're working. Want a glass of wine?"

"Sure, that sounds lovely with the antipasto." She made her way to his coffee table where their books, notes, and pencils sprawled. Off to the side, he'd placed a mortar and pestle, just in case she needed to work with herbs to try something out. He had everything ready for her, anticipating her every need.

Well, not *every* need.

She sat down on the floor, ready to get her mind off Noah and her needs and onto North's blindness. Noah came to her side and sat next to her, two glasses of wine in his hands. She took one and nodded her thanks.

"To discovery," he whispered, the look in his eyes telling her far more than his words.

She licked her suddenly dry lips and touched the rim of her glass to his. "To discovery," she rasped out.

His gaze never left hers as he took a drink. She did the same, gulping hers so she could quench her parched throat. This wolf, oh this wolf, he was going to be the end of her for sure.

"To the books?" she asked, her voice shaky.

He gave her a look that told her he knew exactly what affect he had on her then started to read the text in front of him. Emeline swallowed hard, set down her glass, and then got to work.

She'd read over her own books hundreds of times it seemed and found nothing to help North. It hurt her to no end knowing she couldn't help her friend. There had to be a way.

Caym had used a spell within the Pack's inner circle that was meant to maim and even kill. North had been in the crossfire, thus losing his sight. However, there hadn't been any sort of wound. Physically, his eyes were perfect. There hadn't been a cut or scrape. Nothing had actually *touched* his eyes, or anything in his brain, that could have caused this.

No, it was magic.

And magic could be changed and spells reversed.

There would be a price, Emeline knew, but that was something she was prepared to deal with. She walked the fine line of magic, light versus dark, without actually being a witch. Because she was an elder, her long life had given her the ability to connect to the moon goddess on a level that not everyone understood. She herself didn't quite understand it. Sometimes, when the wind brushed along her just right, she could hear the moon goddess's song. Unlike Lexi and Logan, who had actually heard the moon goddess speak to them, Emeline could hear only whispers, vague ideas of the next step in her process.

That accounted for most of her daydreaming to some, she thought. She'd stand in the middle of a forest, her ear bent to the wind, listening to the song of the goddess. None of the other elders had that level of connection, and some had been resentful, Meryl especially, but as Emeline had no control over it, she didn't feel too bad about it.

No, she used her gift to help others.

It was all she could do in thanks.

So now, here she was, head bent over another book, magic unlike a witch's running through her veins and a small prayer in her heart.

Noah shifted, his arm pressing into hers slightly. She pressed back, leaning into him, taking that small guilty pleasure.

He bent and kissed the top of her head, sending warmth through her body.

It was such a small thing, a slight touch here, a sweet kiss there, but she relished it. Craved it.

She didn't want to let it go.

Not ever.

"Shit. What about this?"

Emeline started at Noah's words then looked at the book in front of him. He wrapped an arm around her shoulders, pulling her closer. She inhaled his musky scent then promptly forgot her need for him as she read the words in front of her.

"Oh goddess, this could work!"

Noah kissed her temple and squeezed her tight. "It's a spell to counteract the dark. The only caveat is that it takes direct contact with the optical nerve." Noah cursed. "I'm not proficient enough for what this eye surgery would entail. I've assisted North with it once, but I've never done anything like that on my own. I'm still learning. But with Hannah's help, I think we could do it." He and North might run only a clinic, but they'd learned as much of modern medicine as they could. They needed to heal all types of injures humans could not be allowed to see, so it made sense that Noah would know about this type of procedure.

"You can. You'd have to take your time and learn how to do it before we even go to North. Plus, according to this, it will take me at least six months to brew the right spell."

"But we can do this. It'll work." Excitement filled Noah's voice, and it was all Emeline could do not to throw her arms around him and kiss him senseless.

"It will work. We can't get North's hopes up, though. So we keep it to ourselves while we're learning and then let them all know so they're prepared."

"Sounds like a plan to me. Holy shit, Em, we did it."

"Well, we're going to."

He smiled then kissed her softly, pulling back with a groan. "Let's get you some food, put these books away, and take the night off." He ran a fingertip under her eyes. "We both need the rest."

"That sounds like a plan."

They picked up their mess and sank into the cushions of the couch, gorging on antipasto and the small sandwiches Noah had made. Emeline leaned into him, enjoying the small comfort.

"Can you tell me about Jeffery?"

Emeline sat up, her sandwich forgotten. "What?"

Noah cursed then sat up as well, taking her plate from her hand and setting it on the coffee table. "I meant to be smoother about that. Shit, I'm sorry, Em."

"Why? Why do you want to know?"

A strange look passed over his face, and then he sighed. "I want to know more about you. Jeffery was your mate and a heavy part of your past. I...I just want to know you."

Emeline licked her lips, her mind going in a hundred different directions. She didn't want to talk about Jeffery. She wanted him firmly in the past. She couldn't think about what she'd lost when she sat next to the man she wanted now.

It wasn't a stain on Jeffery's memory for her to want another man. It had been a years since he'd passed, but it was difficult for her to speak about him in any sense.

That's why she had to do it.

"He wasn't my full mate," she began. "We never completed the mating process."

Noah nodded, urging her to continue. He took her hand, and her wolf steadied, ready for her to speak.

"My father never liked him. You see Jeffery was a submissive wolf. A strong submissive wolf, but not high ranking. My father was a purist. He wanted only the best for me and refused to believe fate would give me something as useless as a weak mate."

Noah growled, and she held up her free hand.

"My father was an idiot. I know that. I knew that then. I was ready to run away with Jeffery, but he wanted to prove himself worthy." She let out a sigh. "Only I didn't know that at the time.

You see, when my father found out I was going to mate Jeffery anyway, he locked me away and told Jeffery I wanted nothing to do with him. I'd been chained in the basement and broke my fingers trying to release myself, but I couldn't. Jeffery left the den thinking I had rejected him and went to fight another war for another Pack. Instead of fighting and coming home a hero, he died at the hands of another wolf. He was a submissive. He was never supposed to fight in that war, but my father made him."

"Oh, Em, I'm sorry, baby." He cupped her face, and she turned her head, kissing his palm.

She didn't shed a tear. Not this time. She'd moved on from Jeffery in the years past, but it still wasn't an easy conversation to have.

"What happened to your father?"

Emeline sighed. "A former Alpha, Kade's grandfather, had him executed in a Pack circle. He was a traitor."

"Shit, Em. Damn. I don't know what to say."

She shrugged. "It's been over for centuries, Noah. Now you know my past, but you also need to know that it won't direct my future. I'm not the same person I once was."

He smiled then. "I know. You're strong, Em. That's one of the things I like about you."

She sighed, her heart breaking. "I'm not the same person, meaning I won't stand by and ruin something for you."

He frowned. "What are you talking about?"

She pulled away, unable to tell him the words she needed to with him touching her. She stood, wringing her hands in front of her. "I don't think I can be with you. Not when you have the chance to mate with someone else. I won't take that chance of a lifetime away from you."

Hurt splashed across Noah's face, and he stood as well. "What are you saying, Em?"

Her heart quivered, her wolf howling. Oh how she wanted this man. Her wolf craved him. Something in her heart warmed at the thought of him, but she couldn't be so cruel as to ruin his chance at happiness.

Noah growled low. "Emeline. You're wrong."

"I'm not. You need to be with your mate."

"Emeline, baby, *you're* my mate."

Her wolf howled in triumph, and something buried deep unlocked within her. She blinked into Noah's gold-rimmed eyes before her knees went weak and

her vision blackened, her body
falling to the floor.

# CHAPTER SIX

Noah caught her before she hit her head against the table and held her close.

Well, fuck.

That hadn't been the reaction he'd been hoping for when he told her they were mates.

In fact, that wasn't one of any of the reactions he'd thought of.

He'd imagined smiling, kissing, or even screaming.

Maybe a few hits if she was really upset and or a shake of her head if she couldn't believe it.

Not passing out.

He cradled her to his body and made his way to his room. He could have left her on the couch, but he wanted to make sure she had space.

Hell, he wanted her in his room, his bed. Even if it was just until she recuperated and ran out of his life forever, he wanted her head on his pillow, her hair splayed around her like a halo.

He set her down on the bed, careful not to jostle her. He checked her pulse and eyes and knew she'd only fainted and wasn't in any real danger. Even so, if she didn't wake up soon, he'd call Hannah. Not that he necessarily wanted to explain that Emeline had passed out because he'd mentioned they were mates.

Yeah, not the best reaction.

At all.

He sat down next to her, brushing her hair from her face. Hell, he didn't know what to do. He knew he wanted her for the rest of their lives. He wanted to form the mating bond, connect their souls, and follow their path to a future.

None of that mattered though. Not when he wasn't sure why she'd reacted like that or if she even felt him as hers in the first place.

Fuck.

Everything was slipping through his fingers, and if he didn't find a way to reach out and grab his future, everything would be lost.

Emeline shifted on the bed, her eyelids fluttering open.

Noah sucked in a breath then hovered over her, cupping her face

"Em," he whispered.

"Noah? Why am I lying down?" she asked, her voice soft and so damn sexy.

"You passed out in the living room." He brushed his thumb over her lips, unable to keep from touching her.

"Where am I?"

"My bedroom," he rasped out.

She sat up quickly, slamming her head into his jaw. He shot to his feet, running a hand over his face as he blinked away stars.

"Crap, I'm sorry," Emeline said, rubbing her head.

He shook his head then sat back down, tucking a strand of hair behind her ear. "I'm fine. It takes more than that to knock a few teeth loose. How's your head?"

"I'll be fine." She closed her eyes then popped them back open. "Mate? You said I'm your mate?"

Noah swallowed hard then nodded. "You're mine, Emeline. I've known since the first time I saw you. That mating urge clicked, and I had to fight off my instincts to just claim you and call you my own." He gave her a sheepish smile. "Wolves, right?"

Tears filled her eyes, and Noah broke.

No.

No. It couldn't be. She couldn't be letting him down. Damn it.

Fate didn't work this way.

It *couldn't* work this way.

Her hand crept up to between her breasts over her heart. "Noah...I..."

He put his fingers over her lips. "No, don't say I'm not yours. I *am*. You know it. You might not be able to feel me as your mate, but...but that could be because you're an elder and things work differently. You're mine, Em. Just like I'm yours. I want to spend the rest of my life with you. I want you to move in here, be my mate, my love. I want to watch the world age around us as we work together for the Pack. I want to watch you grow round with our child. I want it all. I don't care if fate screwed up and made it different for us. I want you as mine, Emeline."

She pulled away, tears flowing freely now. "Noah. I *feel* you."

He let out a breath, his body shaking. "Really?"

She nodded. "Really. I couldn't before. Or maybe I did and I didn't know what it meant. My wolf wanted you, I knew, but I didn't know *how* much she wanted you." She smiled. "How much *I* want you."

He crushed his mouth to hers, desperate to have her taste. She gasped then pushed into him, wrapping her arms around his neck. She tasted of wine and Em, a delicate combination.

When he pulled back, his wolf was on edge, ready to claim. Noah, however, wasn't quite ready. Not until they talked more.

"Will you be my mate, Em?"

She blinked up at him then kissed him softly. "This is all so new to me, Noah. I thought my chance at a mate was lost. I haven't given any thought to what I would do if it ever came again."

He let out a breath, his body going numb. She hadn't said yes. Dear goddess, she hadn't said yes.

"Don't give me that look. Please, Noah." Her eyes filled, and she kissed him again. "I want you. I want your body, your heart, your everything. I know I do, but I'm not sure if I'm ready to take that next step." She smiled then let out a shaky breath. "That's a big step. A crazy one without first letting it settle. Do you understand?"

He kissed her again then pulled back, holding his emotions in check. He wasn't sure he completely understood, but he would try. "So you want to mate with me, just not right now?"

Her nose wrinkled, making her look even sexier for some reason. He was officially losing it.

"That makes me sound thoughtless, but I don't know how else to say it. Everything is moving too fast for me right now. I can't just jump into a forever after thinking for years that I would be alone. Years, Noah. Can't we just take it one step at a time knowing we're ending up in the same place? It doesn't feel right to me at the moment to form a mating bond when my emotions are going haywire."

He nodded, disappointed, but relieved nonetheless. She wanted a future, she just needed to stop and think about it first. Knowing her, she'd make a list, go over each step, then work her way to being ready. That was his Em, and honestly, he wouldn't have her any other way.

"I get it. So we continue to date, court...be us. And when you're ready to be my mate in truth, all you have to do is say the word."

She cupped his face, her small smile breaking him again. "I'm sorry, Noah. I just need to understand it all. I...I never thought I'd have this."

He turned his head and kissed her palm. "No need to be sorry. I'm only thinking of the good. As in you actually feel me as your mate to begin with. Goddess, you have no idea how hard it was to think that you didn't think I was yours at all."

"I'm sorry I put you through that. I have no idea why I couldn't make sense of what was going on. I feel like an idiot."

"You shouldn't. It's been a long time." He gave her a wry smile, and she rolled her eyes.

"Calling me old, pup?"

Knowing better, he kissed her nose. "Experienced."

She socked him in the shoulder then squealed as he rolled her so she straddled him, his hands on her hips.

"Watch who you punch," he said, his voice strangled. This might not have been the best move considering his dick currently pressed against the warmth of her pussy through her jeans.

Damn it. He didn't know if he was going to make it. He might have to go rub one off to take the edge off—showing her just how young he really was apparently.

She tilted her head, her eyes glowing gold, then rocked her hips. The friction of the movement about set him off, and he had to grind his teeth.

"Em, baby. Maybe you should get off me so I don't embarrass myself."

She lowered her body, her breasts pressing against his chest. Noah swallowed hard as she licked his lips.

"I want you, Noah. I want you so badly I can barely breathe. But if we're waiting to complete the bond, then I suppose we should wait to have sex as well. Though right now all I can think about is your cock filling me up until I come hard."

Noah groaned, his hips flexing. "We should stop now then."

"Okay," she said as she rocked her hips again, letting out a little gasp.

His grip tightened on her hips, and he thrust up against her clit, his cock throbbing. "You're going to make me come in my jeans, Em. Is that what you want?"

Her head rolled as she nodded then she cupped her breasts, keeping her hips moving at a rhythm sure to get them both off. They were dry humping on each other like teenagers, but fuck, Noah didn't care. He wanted to see her face as she came, hear every catch in her breath.

"Look at me, baby. Look at me when you come."

She opened her eyes, her gaze on his. He cupped her breast, tweaking the nipple, and she let out a gasp, her breath coming in pants. He kept his hips moving against her spread thighs, his dick aching close to bursting.

"Noah, please."

He rolled her nipple through her blouse, and her lips parted, her body flushing as her eyes glowed gold. His balls tightened, and he groaned as he came in his jeans, his own eyes glowing as well.

When they caught their breath, he pulled Emeline to his chest, kissing her softly. “I can’t believe I just came in my jeans like a teenaged boy.” He winced and shifted his legs. “I need to go clean up.”

Emeline laughed then kissed his jaw. “I’m just going to say, even without touching skin to skin—best ever.”

He grinned, his chest puffing out like a rooster. “Oh really?”

She rolled her eyes, pushed on his chest, and then sat up. “Don’t get a big head.” Her eyes drifted to his jean-clad dick, and he snorted. “Well, from what I felt, you’re big enough already.

On that note, I should let you get cleaned up, and I should do the same. At home."

His wolf growled, and he wanted to do the same. He didn't want her to leave, but he knew they were taking things slow. Forcing her to stay with him forever and never letting her out of his sight would probably defeat the purpose.

He nibbled on her lip then rolled off the bed, landing on his feet. He held out a hand. "Would you like me to walk you home?" he asked, knowing they both needed air, or they would be stripping off their clothes in no time.

She shook her head but took his hand. "I'm a quick walk under the moonlight away. And I need to breathe. If I were to let you come home with me...well..."

He grinned then kissed her, letting his lips brush against hers in a gentle caress. "I'll see you in the morning, Em."

"I'd like that."

"You're not getting rid of me any time soon."

"I don't plan on it."

With that, he walked her to his door, but not out of his life.

She was his mate and knew it.

He was one step closer.

Thank the goddess.

*****

Emeline stretched her hands to the ceiling, trying to wake up. She'd tossed and turned the night before, cursing herself for not staying at Noah's. On the other hand, if she'd stayed there, she'd have thrown her plans in the air and mate marked him right then.

Images of her riding him while they wore their clothes filled her mind, and she groaned.

Okay, enough of that. Noah would be there soon, and they would spend the day together. They hadn't really talked about what exactly they would be doing, but she had an idea. The day before had been a day full of surprises and, like their toast had promised, discovery.

While she would have loved to spend the day rolling around in the grass with Noah and learning every inch of him, they had other things to do. Namely, work on the spell for North. Each of them had serious preparation to do, as well as studying up on techniques. It would have been great if she could have told Lexi and North what she and Noah had found, but she hadn't wanted to get Lexi's hopes up.

So when Lexi had called just a few moments before, Emeline lied. No, not lied, she had told the other woman they were still working on it. They were, after all, but she hadn't elaborated. Emeline was just too worried that they'd find out, as she and Noah worked at it, that it wouldn't work and she'd disappoint them when there had been a way to prevent it.

When she and Noah got closer to the end of their timetable, they would tell North, Lexi, and the rest of the Jamensons. There was no way they'd be able to keep their excitement to themselves for long. If the others happened to mention the way she felt, well, then they could attribute it to her new relationship with Noah.

She smiled wide, her cheeks hurting from doing that so much.

Her mate.

Noah was her mate.

She still couldn't quite believe it.

She also couldn't quite believe that she hadn't completed the mating the night before. Even though she would have loved to cement their bond, she knew it was the right decision to wait until she was centered.

And from the way she was feeling at the moment, she knew it wouldn't be that long a wait for either of them.

Thank the goddess.

"Why are you smiling, girl?" Meryl snapped from the doorway she hadn't heard open.

Emeline turned on her heel, cursing herself for not locking the door. While the den was safe now, she still should have made it harder for Meryl and the other elders to come into her home without asking. Before, they had been welcome because there had been no other way. Now, though, Emeline wanted her space.

Well, it was too late now.

Also, the fact that Meryl called her "girl" was not lost on her. Emeline just chose to ignore it. Meryl, being as old and batshit crazy as she was, was also far too set in her ways. There was no pleasing the woman. It had taken Emeline leaving the elder part of the den to start to see it fully.

"I'm happy, Meryl. Good morning. Would you like some tea?"

Meryl snarled. "No, I don't want any tea. I want to know why you're disgracing yourself and the Pack. I smell that pup on you. It's an abomination. That's what it is."

Emeline froze, her eyes wide. "Excuse me?"

"You heard me, girl. Noah isn't for the likes of you. You're an elder. You're not to act like a tramp and screw the little pups in our Pack. You're supposed to stay within our elder den and act accordingly. Fraternizing with the pups is a sin."

Dear goddess, Meryl had officially lost her marbles.

"I don't know where you get by talking to me like that, Meryl. You're an elder, sure, but so am I. I demand the same respect as I give you." She held up her hand when Meryl started to speak. "No, this is *my* home. You don't get to come in here and bully me. First, I can *screw* anyone I want. You don't get to tell me who I share my body with. Second, Noah is of age. We're wolves. Get over it." Funny how she could say that now, but that was neither here nor there. "Third, Noah is my mate, so you better get used to me *fraternizing* with him. Now if that's all you have to say, you can leave."

Meryl paled, but her eyes grew mean. "Mate? How dare you? You've had your mate, and you lost him. You had Jeffery. How could you sully his name with the likes of Noah? What would he say? You've forgotten your so-called love for a man who died for you so you could be with this pup? Shame on you."

Emeline ignored the sting across her heart. She hadn't forgotten Jeffery, but she'd moved on. Damn what Meryl thought.

"We're done here, Meryl. I'm entitled to happiness."

"You're a whore, Emeline. Mark my words, you'll pay for your sins."

Emeline opened the door and growled. "Don't threaten me, Meryl. Go home and wallow in your own misery. I'm done doing the same."

She slammed the door in Meryl's face, this time locking it. As the adrenaline left her, she sank to the floor, tears covering her cheeks.

She was happy. She really was. Noah would make her whole again, just as she was making herself whole.

She loved him.

Oh yes, she loved him and had for a while.

They'd spent over a year side by side, him courting her slowly. She'd had all the time in the world to get used to him in her heart, and he was already there, making himself at home.

She thought of Jeffery and what she'd had with him. It wasn't the same, but it should be.

Noah was hers now, and she would claim him.

In fact, she thought Jeffery would approve of Noah, even like him. That was just the kind of wolf he had been. They might never have completed the mating bond, but he'd been part of her soul and her memories for so long, she could not remember a time when he wasn't there.

"Oh, Jeffery," she whispered, crying happy tears over her new discovery.

Noah's scent hit her hard, and she cursed herself for leaving the back door unlocked just as she'd left the front door. It seemed today was the day for surprises. However, this time, Noah was a welcome one.

She turned to him, a smile on her face, only to see stone.

"Noah?" she asked, her voice soft. "What's wrong?"

His jaw tightened, and he took a step back as she moved toward him. Her heart stuttered, and she blinked.

"Noah?"

"I should have known the reason you weren't ready," he whispered, his voice broken. *Oh goddess, no.* "You'll never be ready." He sighed, his throat working as he swallowed hard. "I only wish you loved me only a fraction as much as you loved Jeffery. I'm sorry to have made you cry. You shouldn't have to deal with the pain of saying goodbye and having to choose. I understand that now. Goodbye, Em," he whispered. With that he turned and walked away, leaving her frozen in his wake.

No, he wasn't supposed to leave. He'd gotten it all wrong. Damn it. She ran behind him, her mouth open to call his name, when something struck her on the back of the head. Blinding pain snapped at her, and she blinked once, twice, before hitting the ground, her world dark.

# CHAPTER SEVEN

Noah found himself in front of Logan and Cailin's door, unable to knock.

She'd cried for a dead man.

Cried and cried and broken him.

He couldn't blame her for her tears. Couldn't blame her for her choice. Mates were everlasting. Finding a second one in a lifetime was almost unheard of. The pain and anguish that came with choosing the second and slowly letting go of the first would be hard for anyone to overcome.

Adam Jamenson had done it and had hurt his second mate, Bay, terribly in the process.

Noah just wished Emeline had done the same.

No, he couldn't quite say that. Not when the pain of what Emeline had gone through, was going through, was too much to bear. Noah hated the fact he'd put her through that.

The door opened, and Cailin stood there, pity on her face.

Damn it, he hated pity.

It was all he could do not to weep like a baby and wish for them to make it better. He knew he could have gone to his parents for comfort, but they hadn't met Emeline yet. He'd been planning on introducing them the next day, actually. Cailin and Logan, though, knew all about Emeline and were her friends. They'd understand the depth of her sorrow and the strength of his own.

"Oh, Noah," Cailin said. "Come on in, honey. We'll get you something to drink." She pulled him in the house, and he shuffled in, numb. "Logan?" she called over her shoulder. "Bring the whiskey."

Logan rambled in, Edward in his arms. He gave one look at Noah then cursed under his breath. "Here, take the baby, I'll get the whiskey."

Noah shook his head. "It's too early for whiskey."

Logan squeezed his shoulder. "When you're in the state you're in, it's never too early for whiskey."

Noah nodded anyway then went to the couch and sat down—well, more like flopped really. He couldn't think about anything more than the tears on Emeline's cheeks and the way she'd said her dead mate's name.

Damn Jeffery.

Cailin plopped Edward in his lap then sat next to them. "Hold the baby. He makes everything better most days."

Noah held Edward close and sighed. "You're right about that, but I don't think even he is strong enough for this."

"Then we'll help with whatever is left," she said simply then leaned her head on his shoulder. Logan came to his other side, set the tumbler of whiskey on the table, and then sat back.

No one spoke, but then again, no one needed to.

"I can't blame her, you know," Noah said.

Cailin straightened. "She rejected you and you're not blaming her?"

Was it a rejection? Or a choice not to feel the pain anymore?

"If she's feeling a fraction of what I am at the thought of not having her in my life, I can't really blame her. She lost someone precious to her, and I can't make that pain go away. I just don't know what to do."

Cailin opened her mouth to speak then looked at Logan. Noah saw the love in both of their eyes and swallowed. The two of them loved each other in every way possible. He was even holding the evidence of that mating. With that, they understood what he was talking about, he was sure. She sighed once more, then sat with him in silence.

He just needed them for support, and then he'd figure out what to do.

The door crashed open, and Maddox ran in, his eyes gold. "Don't you answer your phones?"

Logan stood, his hands ready to turn to claws at the sign of a fight.

Cailin had Edward in her arms and behind Logan to protect their son in a blink of an eye. Noah stood as well, ready to help Maddox in any way possible.

"We put them on silent to help Noah," Cailin answered. "What is it?"

Maddox growled. "Something's wrong. I don't know what." He met Noah's gaze. "I don't have as strong as a connection to Emeline because she's an elder and, therefore, has a kind of barrier around her when it comes to my Omega powers. However, I felt her emotional pain and then a snap. Like something hurt her."

Noah growled. He knew what the first part was, but the second?

That he had no idea.

But he'd find out.

And when he found out who, other than him, had hurt her?

He'd end them.

****

Emeline opened her eyes then shut them tightly as the world went hazy around her. What the hell had hit her upside the head? She tried to touch her temple to relieve some of the ache, only to find herself immobile.

What the heck?

She blinked then looked up at her hands that were chained to the wall.

Oh goddess, what was happening?

She remembered the pain of watching Noah walk away—that sharp pang sliced at her again—then she'd followed him...only to have everything go black. Someone had hit her on the head and taken her here—wherever here was. They'd chained her to the wall with shifter chains, meaning it would take more strength than she possessed to break free. With normal chains, she would have been able to pull them apart relatively easily. However, shifter chains were magically infused and could expand and tighten depending on the form of the shifter.

She'd just have to find another way out.

Her gaze moved over her surroundings, trying to figure out where she was. Best she could figure, whoever had taken her had locked her inside a cave in the rockface in the east of the den. The Redwood den sat between two mountain peaks and one of the main cliffs had numerous small caves.

Between the head injury and whatever spell the chains were laying over her, Emeline couldn't scent who had taken her. It had to be someone within the Pack because they'd been inside the wards, but other than that, she had no clue.

Who had she angered enough that they'd hit her then kidnapped her?

"You're awake. Good."

Emeline's head shot up at the voice, and then she cursed inwardly that she hadn't thought of the danger that had lurked around her for so long.

"Meryl."

"I told you to leave him, and what do you do? You run after him." Meryl sat on a rock in front of where Emeline sat chained.

The other woman's eyes were bright with madness, the gold glow that came from her wolf lighting then dimming, as if her wolf was in and out of control.

Not good.

There was a reason that not all wolves lived to Meryl's age. Between wars, battles, and dominance fights, the strength that came from surviving centuries put a strain on one's sanity. It took a mating bond—or in Emeline's case, a true connection to the moon goddess—not to lose control completely. Emeline had thought she'd follow the path so many others had and fade away. That was before she'd met Noah. Meryl had always straddled the edge of sanity, and it seemed that she'd taken the leap into batshit crazy.

"Meryl. How do you think this is a good idea?"

Meryl lifted a lip in a snarl then smacked Emeline across the face. Hard.

Emeline squeezed her eyes shut to keep the dizziness at bay then opened them again to watch what Meryl would do next.

"I don't understand how the moon goddess and fate can bless you with two mates when I've met *none*." Meryl stood in a jerky movement then paced in front of Emeline.

Emeline tried to wiggle her wrists free from the manacles, but it was no use. She was well and truly chained. She only prayed that Noah or another wolf would know she was in trouble. Not that she wanted to be the damsel in distress, but right then, she couldn't exactly move to save herself. At least not yet.

"I'm sorry you haven't found your mate yet. There's still time, Meryl." Not likely since the older wolf had gone off the deep end, but Emeline needed time to formulate a plan other than wait around to be saved.

"There's no time," Meryl spat. "There's never been any time. And it doesn't matter anyway. Fate took the only man I loved and gave him to you."

"What? What...do you mean?" *Meryl loved Noah?*

"From the look in your eyes, you're an idiot. I loved Jeffery. He was going to be *mine*. Then you had to walk up to him and show him what fate wanted. Well, fuck fate. Jeffery was *mine*."

"I...I never knew. I'm so sorry, Meryl." She was honest in that. To find out the man you loved was fated to another had to hurt in so many ways, but that didn't give the other woman the excuse to chain Emeline to a cliff wall.

"I thought I could keep him away from you. I even had your father help me, but it wasn't enough."

Shocked, Emeline could only stare. Meryl and her father had worked together to keep her and Jeffery apart? What the hell?

"Then when you decided to be with him anyway, well, there was nothing else I could do. You see, with you in the picture, Jeffery didn't want me. He would have *loved* me without you there. But then you muddled his brains with your violet eyes and soft words. Well, fuck you, Emeline. You never deserved him. And because you *ruined* him, I had to make sure no one had him."

Emeline licked her lips, her heart thudding loudly in her ears. "What are you saying, Meryl? What did you do?"

Meryl raised her chin, that manic gleam to her eyes

brightening even more. "I helped your father chain you to the basement, much like you're chained now. Of course, they're different chains since you destroyed the last ones in your desperate and bloody attempts to free yourself. Then I sent Jeffery away to war. It wasn't hard. He already thought you'd chosen anyone over him. You never deserved him anyway. He was *mine*. And if I couldn't have him, no one could."

Emeline's jaw dropped, her wolf raging inside.

Jeffery had died, and everything that had happened since was because of this woman's petty jealousy.

"You've got to be fucking kidding me. How could you do that? How could you send someone you say you loved to his death?"

Meryl slapped her hard again, but Emeline didn't close her eyes this time. There was no telling what Meryl would do next.

"You bitch. You don't understand true love. We would have had an amazing life together, and then you had to show another path. That path was a lie. A lie! He should have been with *me*."

Everything started to make sense then. The years of living cut off within the elder's part of the den because of Meryl. Meryl had ruled that area with an iron fist because of her age, and the rest of them had given in because they didn't know any better. Emeline had taken the brunt of Meryl's judgments and all because Meryl was a jealous bitch.

Well, no more.

"I can't believe you did all of that, Meryl. You had no right."

"I had every right. And now I will make sure you never feel what you did for that man again. You should have stayed in your little house and away from the other wolves. But no, you had to go and prove yourself worthy to the fucking Alpha and his family. You were nothing, and you should have stayed that way. Now you think you're better than the rest of us. You even found *another* mate. How is that fair? Huh? Well, no bother, Noah left you, and when I'm done with you, he'll never have you again."

Emeline froze, her wolf growling. "Don't you dare touch Noah."

"I won't hurt him. I won't even look at him. No, I'm going to kill you right here on the side of this cliff. Then I will make it look like Noah did it so he'll face judgment from the Alpha and his brothers. When he dies, everything you've ever tainted will be gone. Then I can finally be at peace."

No. Noah would *not* be touched. He would *not* face any form of judgment from the Alpha. That would be dealt with later. Now, though, Meryl needed to be stopped. Emeline was done lying down and taking whatever came at her. She was *done* living by Meryl's dictates. She wanted to find Noah, tell him the truth about the tears he'd seen, and then mark him as her mate.

She wanted all of that, and damn it, she'd get it.

Emeline pulled at the manacles with all her strength. The metal bit into her wrists, and a trail of blood ran down her arms.

Meryl grinned, and Emeline's wolf rose to the surface, ready to claw that grin right off the bitch's face.

Emeline let her wolf rise even further and shifted her hands, forcing her claws to rip through her fingers, squeezing down on the manacle. Meryl's eyes opened wide, but Emeline ignored them for the moment. Oh, she'd get to the other woman soon. Right then, she just needed to get free. Letting the magic of the moon goddess wash over her—something she tried hard not to take advantage of, as being in debt to a goddess was never a good idea—she growled. Her body shook, her strength increasing as she pulled harder.

Blood oozed from her cuts, but, again, she ignored it. She pulled one more time, and the manacles broke free of the chains then hit the ground.

Meryl scrambled to her feet, her own claws popping from her fingertips. Emeline pounced, knocking the woman to the ground.

"Don't you dare, Meryl. You've hurt me and those I love for the last time." She punched the woman in the face, knocking Meryl's head into the ground. Hard.

The sound soothed her wolf. Somewhat.

Meryl clawed at her, but Emeline was faster. She took the other woman by the neck then hit her again. This time, Meryl's eyes rolled to the back of her head, as she lost consciousness.

Thank the goddess.

"Emeline!"

Emeline turned on her heel and left Meryl where she lay. Noah held out his arms, and she jumped into them, letting her claws retract back into her hands at the same time. He squeezed her hard, and she wrapped her legs around his waist, kissing his cheeks, his forehead, his nose, his lips.

"Oh thank the goddess you're here," she whispered then kissed him again.

"It would seem to me that she didn't really need us," Logan said as he walked past her and Noah on his way to Meryl.

"Yeah, looks like she saved herself," Maddox added as he followed Logan.

Noah's hands ran up and down her back, his heart thudding hard against hers. "Are you okay? You're bleeding. Let me take care of you."

"I will be fine. Let me hold you for a moment first." She rested her forehead against his, her wolf finally calming. "I'm so sorry, Noah."

"No, no. Don't be. I'm sorry I left." He choked out a breath. "I'm so fucking sorry I left."

She cupped his face, ignoring the other two wolves taking care of Meryl behind her. "I wasn't crying for Jeffery. I was saying goodbye. I was happy, Noah. I love you so much. I don't want to wait anymore. Please, if you'll still have me, please be my mate."

Noah kissed her softly, letting his lips press against hers in a gentle caress. "I love you so fucking much, Em. You never have to apologize for loving Jeffery before me. I'm sorry I was such a dumbass. Let me take you home, and then we'll start on forever. What do you say?"

Emeline traced her finger along his jaw then nodded, her cheeks hurting from smiling so wide. "I say yes, Noah. Yes, yes, yes, *yes*!"

He didn't put her down, and she let him carry her. Both of their wolves needed the comfort, and since she'd saved herself, his dominant wolf needed the extra reassurance that she was truly okay.

She trusted Maddox and Logan to take care of Meryl, and when the time was right, she'd deal with the ramifications of what had happened. Right then though, she wanted to stay in Noah's arms and know that she was safe.

Safe, strong, and his.

# CHAPTER EIGHT

Noah let out a breath, his hands gripping the pedestal sink as if it were a lifeline. He'd almost lost her. He walked out of her home and sulked because he'd been a fucking idiot. Yes, he knew he would have gone back and groveled. Fought for what he wanted. But the sheer shock of what he thought had been her crying for another man pummeled him.

Because he left, she'd been hurt. She'd been forced to listen to Meryl's tirade, and if she hadn't been strong enough, she could have died because of him.

How the hell was he going to make that up to her?

Small hands fell over his hips, and he sighed, his wolf soothed for the first time since he'd walked into her home that morning. His wolf had raged, howled, and clawed throughout the day, even when he'd found her in that cave relatively unharmed. The sight of her blood, and the fact that he hadn't been able to do anything to protect her, hadn't helped his dominant wolf.

Her touch, though, helped in ways he was only beginning to understand.

He turned in her arms, wrapping his arms around her. She didn't even reach his chin, and he and his wolf loved her compact size. She fit against him just right, and if he had his way, he'd never let her go again.

That might be a problem in the future when it came to actually letting her out of his sight, but he'd cross that barrier when he had to. For now, he'd be content with her in his arms and, soon, in his bed.

They'd come to his home straight from the cave, his wolf leading the charge and the man following close behind. He'd cleaned her wounds, though she healed quickly on her own. Whatever she'd done by connecting to the moon goddess expedited her already quick healing from being a wolf. Still, he'd checked over every inch of her.

Hence, why she stood in only his robe, the gap in the front parted so he could see the curve of her breasts. His cock filled and his wolf howled. He took her hands and drew her into his bedroom. They stood at the end of the bed, her back to the bed as he faced her, his gaze on hers as he tried to drink in every inch of her, cementing this moment, this woman, this mate in his heart and mind forever.

He not only wanted to fill her, he wanted to taste her, fuck her, make love to her, and feel her in every way.

Emeline was his.

“When you look at me like that, I feel like I’m the only woman in the world,” she whispered. Her hands went to the bottom of his shirt, lifting slowly. He raised his arms, aiding her so he stood in only his jeans.

She swallowed hard, her finger going to his nipple ring. "I've had dreams about this nipple ring," she murmured.

He quirked a grin and cupped her face. "Really? What do these dreams entail?"

She licked her lips, and he imagined that tongue on his nipple ring....on his dick. Oh, yeah...soon.

"Oh, just a little of this," she flicked her tongue against the metal ring, sending heat straight to his cock, "a little of that." Her teeth clamped down on the ring, and she tugged, shocking a groan out of him.

"Holy shit, baby, you need to do that again."

She blinked up at him. "This?" She tugged again, this time her hand squeezing the length of his cock through his jeans. He sucked in a breath, holding on to that last thread of control.

He gripped her chin then crushed his mouth to hers, sucking her bottom lip into his mouth before tangling his tongue with hers. Her hand went from his other nipple to his back, her fingernails digging into his skin. The slight sting pushed him over the edge, and he pulled his mouth away, growling.

"Robe. Off. Now."

Her eyes widened at his tone, and then she undid the belt, letting the robe pool at her feet. Her chest rose as she took a deep breath, and he took one as well, inhaling her sweet scent that went straight to his cock. Her nipples tightened under his gaze, the dusty rose darkening against the paleness of her skin.

"I'm going to lick those pretty breasts of yours, Em, and then I'm going to taste each and every bit of you. After you come on my tongue, I'm going to fill you with my cock and ride you until we both come. My seed will fill you, and I'll sink my fangs into your neck, marking you as mine. Then you'll do the same, and our mating bond will form, making me yours just as much as you're mine. How does that sound?"

Her throat worked as she swallowed hard. "Noah...I didn't know you were such a dirty talker."

He grinned then cupped her breast, molding the heavy weight in his palm before pinching her nipple. She let out a shocked gasp, arching into him, pushing her breast firmer against his hand. He did the same to her other breast, loving the way her nipples reddened under his attention.

"I like telling you what's going to happen. You might think

my tongue is wicked, but you haven't seen anything yet."

She let out a small laugh, and he kissed her softly, wanting her taste. Craving it. He trailed kisses down her jaw and up again to the soft spot behind her ear. She shuddered in his hold, gripping his biceps. He licked and nibbled down her neck to the spot where it met her shoulder, grazing his teeth along the juncture.

"This is where I'm going to mark you. Tomorrow, when we're both finally able to walk again after making love all night, you'll wear your hair up so everyone can see my mark. I'll show off mine as well, and the world will know what happened tonight."

"Noah, please, you're going to make me come just from your words alone."

He knelt before her, kissing her belly, her hips. "I'm going to make you come more than once tonight, baby. Put your hands on my shoulders so you don't fall."

"Noah..."

"Em." His voice held no room for saying no.

She put her hands on his shoulders.

He spread her legs slightly then trailed a finger down the soft curls on her mound. Her legs shook a bit, and he grinned.

Oh yes, this was going to be fun.

He leaned forward, darting his tongue out so he could lick the hood over her clit. She gasped, pressing her pussy closer to his face.

He looked up, and her violet eyes darkened as she stared at him. "Since you asked so nicely, baby. Hold on."

She licked her lips again, and he buried his face in her curls.

"Noah," she gasped.

He licked and sucked around her clit, scraping his teeth down gently. Her nails dug into his shoulders, and he laid the flat of his tongue along her opening. Careful to keep her balanced, he lifted one of her legs slightly so he could have better access before spearing her with two fingers. Her head fell back, and he thrust in and out of her, curling his fingers over the soft bundle of nerves.

When her inner walls tightened, clamping down on his fingers, he bit down on her clit, sending her straight over the edge. She screamed his name, and he felt more than saw her knees give out.

Before she could fall back on the bed, he was up and had his arms around her, slanting his lips over hers. She kissed him back fully, wrapping her arms around him.

When he pulled back, they were both breathless, and his cock was rock hard. “Fuck, I love your taste, Em. I want you again, but I don’t think I can wait.”

Her hands went to the button of his jeans, popping the top one. “Let me return the favor. I want you on my tongue.”

He groaned, sucking in her bottom lip. “Next time. I don’t want to come for the first time down your throat. I’d rather fill your pussy and start the mating bond.”

There were two steps to the mating bond, the first being to fill the woman with the man’s seed, mating the humans. The mating mark would cement the bond between their wolves.

She rolled her eyes then pushed him back slightly. “Fine. Next time. As in later tonight. Now get in me, Noah. I’m your elder. You need to listen to me.”

Noah snorted. "Really? You're going to use that as a way to get what you want in bed?"

She traced her finger along his chin. "I'll use it any way I please. Now take off those jeans and fuck me."

He groaned then stripped off his jeans as quickly as he could without falling face first on the bed. Then he gripped her hips and flipped her so she landed on her hands and knees, letting out a little squeal.

"Noah!"

"This way first. Then I want to see your eyes when you come around my cock." He ran his hand over her hips and ass, knowing he'd have a century or four to learn every inch of her. He couldn't wait.

As he pressed the head of his cock against her pussy, they both shuddered a breath. Then he sank into her inch by agonizing inch.

When he was balls deep, he bent over her, his lips on her shoulder.

"Fuck, baby. You feel so good."

She wiggled on his dick. "Move, Noah. Please, for the love of the goddess, *move*."

Since she asked…

He pulled out slowly then hammered back in, thrusting in and out of her as her hips moved back to meet him with every movement. Damn, she was so tight. So his.

Just when his balls tightened, and he knew he was ready to blow, he pulled out then moved her to her back.

She smiled then wrapped her legs around his waist as he sank into her once more. He tangled his fingers with hers, their gazes never leaving each other as he pumped his hips.

"Mine," he whispered.

"Mine," she whispered back.

With that, he came, his seed filling her as she came around his cock. He felt the first part of the bond snap into place, their souls intertwining. She moved her head to the side, baring her neck. Needing no further invitation, he sank fangs into her neck, marking her as his for all eternity. His wolf howled in triumph, his mate underneath him humming in pleasure. He licked the wound closed then moved his head so she could mark him as well. When her fangs bit into him, he gasped, the final part of the bond forming.

His mate.

His Emeline.

His forever.

Once they caught their breath, he pulled out of her then brought them to their sides, their foreheads resting on one another.

"Mine forever, Emeline," he whispered, knowing he was

repeating himself, but he couldn't help it. He might not have waited centuries for this moment like Emeline had, but everything he'd done before this brought him here.

"Yours, Noah. Thank you for finding me, for being the wolf you are on the hunt for my heart. I love you." She kissed him then, a soft brush of their lips.

She was right. He'd hunted her heart and come out the victor. Now he had an eternity to revel in his prize.

In his Emeline.

# EPILOGUE

*Six Months Later*

"This is going to work," Emeline whispered to herself. This had to work.

Noah wrapped his arms around her waist, and she leaned into him, his presence calming her like nothing else could.

The past six months had been a blur of mating heat, promises, and new beginnings. She and Noah had their hands on each other in some way for most of the day, like most new matings, unable to be apart for long.

When they weren't wrapped up in each other, they'd been working…and moving on. Before Meryl could be sentenced by Kade and the others, she'd found a way to take herbs to put her to sleep forever. So instead of facing her crimes, she exacted justice by her own hand. Emeline didn't feel much for that, other than the tragic loss of so many years because of one woman's selfishness.

That was behind them now.

Hopefully, the other project they'd spent so much time and effort on would soon prove fruitful as well. The potion that had taken six months to get just right was ready. Noah had taken every spare moment when he wasn't with Emeline learning the surgical procedure he'd performed four hours prior with the help of Hannah, their Healer, and Emeline at his side. Lexi had been in the room as well, the woman stronger than anyone Emeline had ever known. She'd refused to leave North's side at any time, even though they all knew seeing her mate like that would place a terrible burden on her wolf.

It hadn't mattered though. North had come through it and Lexi had as well.

Well, at least mostly. He was still asleep, the effect of the drugs and the spell hopefully wearing off soon. Physically, North looked as though nothing had been done. Between Hannah and North's werewolf healing, he looked none the worse for wear. Most of the Jamensons remained in the waiting area to give North privacy to recover, but Lexi, Parker, Isabelle, Emeline, and Noah were at his side.

He should be waking up at any moment, and then they would know if their spell had worked.

If this didn't work...well...Emeline couldn't think about that.

Not yet.

North rustled on the bed, and everyone stiffened. Lexi gave Isabelle to Parker, the boy handling his little sister like a pro, and then went to her mate's side. Emeline started to move as well, but Noah held her back. She looked over her shoulder at him, and he shook his head.

Yes, Lexi needed to be the one North saw first—if he could indeed see.

"North?" Lexi whispered as she cupped her mate's cheek.

"Lex?" North rasped out. He fluttered his eyelids, and Emeline sucked in a breath, her heart thudding.

"Baby, open your eyes. Tell me what you see."

It took a moment, but he opened his eyes then frowned. The sight sent Emeline back against Noah.

"I only see blurs," North whispered, his voice raw. "It's better than before, but...but I don't know."

Damn it.

Noah kissed her temple, and she brushed away a tear. It hadn't worked. All of their hope had rested on this moment, and North still couldn't see.

Lexi sniffed as tears slid down her cheeks, her hand still on her mate's cheek. "It's okay, baby. We'll give it time. You've only just woken up."

Isabelle let out a cry, and Lexi turned, holding out her arms. "Give me your sister, Parker. I think she wants her daddy."

When Parker did, Emeline stared at North, who kept blinking, his jaw firm. He looked so lost, so sad. And there was nothing more she could do about it.

"Here, baby, hold your daughter. She wants you."

North held out his arms, and Lexi placed Isabelle in his arms, brushing a kiss on her forehead before she leaned back. North shifted then looked down at the baby in his arms, his throat working as he swallowed hard.

"Isabelle..."

Emeline straightened as North blinked once, twice. Then threw his back and laughed.

"What?" Lexi asked, her hand on North's shoulder. "What is it?"

"Our daughter looks just like you, Lexi." Tears fell down his cheeks, and Lexi looked ready to pass out. Parker ran to his mom's side and helped her sit on the edge of the bed.

"You can see?" she asked, and Emeline had to force herself not to run to the edge of the bed and join in their family moment.

"I can see," North said in awe. "It's fitting that my first sight is Isabelle, don't you think? Daddy's little girl is the most precious thing."

Emeline burst into tears with the rest of the people in the room and turned into Noah's arms. "We did it."

He cupped her face, his eyes shimmering with tears as well. "We did, Em."

"Thank you for being mine," she whispered, her heart so full she could barely breathe.

"I would have hunted to the ends of the earth for you, Em."

She kissed him then, her heart in her throat. Noah was hers, and she wouldn't have it any other way.

The End

*Coming Next: Wicked Wolf*

# A Note from Carrie Ann

Thank you so much for reading **THE HUNTED HEART**. I do hope if you liked this story, that you would please leave a review. Not only does a review spread the word to other readers, they let us authors know if you'd like to see more stories like this from us. I love hearing from readers and talking to them when I can. If you want to make sure you know what's coming next from me, you can sign up for my newsletter at www.CarrieAnnRyan.com; follow me on twitter at @CarrieAnnRyan, or like my Facebook page. I also have a Facebook Fan Club where we have trivia, chats, and other goodies. You guys are the reason I get to do what I do and I thank you.

Make sure you're signed up for my MAILING LIST so you can know when the next releases are available as well as find giveaways and FREE READS.

The Hunted Heart was originally found in the Dark Fates Anthology where we had the pleasure of writing sexy novellas about characters we'd found in our series. Emeline had been with me since the middle of the series and I knew her hero had to be special. I'm not ending the Redwood Pack series in truth with this as I have Wicked Wolf coming in Jan 2015. As part of the 1001 Dark Nights series as well, it's going to be a blast. Plus, the Redwoods are continuing in the Talon Pack series. So more wolves!

If you don't want to wait for more Redwood Pack books, I also have my Montgomery Ink, Talon Pack, and Dante's Circle series going in full swing now so there's always a Carrie Ann book on the horizon!

Thank you so much for going on this journey with me and I do hope you enjoyed my Redwood Pack series. Without you readers, I wouldn't be where I am today.

Thank you again for reading and I do hope to see you again.

**Redwood Pack Series:**

Book 1: An Alpha's Path
Book 2: A Taste for a Mate
Book 3: Trinity Bound
Book 3.5: A Night Away
Book 4: Enforcer's Redemption
Book 4.5: Blurred Expectations
Book 4.7: Forgiveness
Book 5: Shattered Emotions
Book 6: Hidden Destiny
Book 6.5: A Beta's Haven
Book 7: Fighting Fate
Book 7.5 Loving the Omega

Book 7.7: The Hunted Heart
Book 8: Wicked Wolf

# About Carrie Ann and her Books

New York Times and USA Today Bestselling Author Carrie Ann Ryan never thought she'd be a writer. Not really. No, she loved math and science and even went on to graduate school in chemistry. Yes, she read as a kid and devoured teen fiction and Harry Potter, but it wasn't until someone handed her a romance book in her late teens that she realized that there was something out there just for her. When another author suggested she use the voices in her head for good and not evil, The Redwood Pack and all her other stories were born.

Carrie Ann is a bestselling author of over twenty novels and novellas and has so much more on her mind (and on her spreadsheets *grins*) that she isn't planning on giving up her dream anytime soon.

www.CarrieAnnRyan.com

**Redwood Pack Series:**
Book 1: An Alpha's Path
Book 2: A Taste for a Mate
Book 3: Trinity Bound
Book 3.5: A Night Away
Book 4: Enforcer's Redemption
Book 4.5: Blurred Expectations
Book 4.7: Forgiveness
Book 5: Shattered Emotions
Book 6: Hidden Destiny
Book 6.5: A Beta's Haven
Book 7: Fighting Fate
Book 7.5 Loving the Omega
Book 7.7: The Hunted Heart
Book 8: Wicked Wolf

**The Talon Pack (Following the Redwood Pack Series):**
Book 1: Tattered Loyalties
Book 2: An Alpha's Choice
Book 3: Mated in Mist (Coming in 2016)

**The Redwood Pack Volumes:**
Redwood Pack Vol 1
Redwood Pack Vol 2
Redwood Pack Vol 3
Redwood Pack Vol 4
Redwood Pack Vol 5
Redwood Pack Vol 6

**Montgomery Ink:**
Book 0.5: Ink Inspired
Book 0.6: Ink Reunited
Book 1: Delicate Ink
Book 1.5 Forever Ink
Book 2: Tempting Boundaries
Book 3: Harder than Words
Book 4: Written in Ink

**The Branded Pack Series:**
**(Written with Alexandra Ivy)**
Books 1 & 2: Stolen and Forgiven
Books 3 & 4: Abandoned and Unseen

**Dante's Circle Series:**
Book 1: Dust of My Wings
Book 2: Her Warriors' Three Wishes
Book 3: An Unlucky Moon
The Dante's Circle Box Set (Contains Books 1-3)
Book 3.5: His Choice
Book 4: Tangled Innocence
Book 5: Fierce Enchantment
Book 6: An Immortal's Song (Coming in 2016)

**Holiday, Montana Series:**
Book 1: Charmed Spirits
Book 2: Santa's Executive
Book 3: Finding Abigail
The Holiday Montana Box Set (Contains Books 1-3)
Book 4: Her Lucky Love

Book 5: Dreams of Ivory

**Tempting Signs Series:**
Finally Found You

# Excerpt: Delicate Ink

**From New York Times Bestselling Author Carrie Ann Ryan's Montgomery Ink**

"If you don't turn that fucking music down, I'm going to ram this tattoo gun up a place no one on this earth should ever see."

Austin Montgomery lifted the needle from his client's arm so he could hold back a rough chuckle. He let his foot slide off the pedal so he could keep his composure. Dear Lord, his sister Maya clearly needed more coffee in her life.

Or for someone to turn down the fucking music in the shop.

"You're not even working, Maya. Let me have my tunes," Sloane, another artist, mumbled under his breath. Yeah, he didn't yell it. Didn't need to. No one wanted to yell at Austin's sister. The man might be as big as a house and made of pure muscle, but no one messed with Maya.

Not if they wanted to live.

"I'm sketching, you dumbass," Maya sniped, even though the smile in her eyes belied her wrath. His sister loved Sloane like a brother. Not that she didn't have enough brothers and sisters to begin with, but the Montgomerys always had their arms open for strays and spares.

Austin rolled his eyes at the pair's antics and stood up from his stool, his body aching from being bent over for too long. He refrained from saying that aloud as Maya and Sloane would have a joke for that. He usually preferred to have the other person in bed—or in the kitchen, office, doorway, etc—bent over, but that wasn't where he would allow his mind to go. As it was, he was too damn old to be sitting in that position for too long, but he wanted to get this sleeve done for his customer.

"Hold on a sec, Rick," he said to the man in the chair. "Want juice or anything? I'm going to stretch my legs and make sure Maya doesn't kill Sloane." He winked as he said it, just in case his client didn't get the joke.

People could be so touchy when siblings threatened each other with bodily harm even while they smiled as they said it.

"Juice sounds good," Rick slurred, a sappy smile on his face. "Don't let Maya kill you."

Rick blinked his eyes open, the adrenaline running through his system giving him the high that a few patrons got once they were in the chair for a couple hours. To Austin, there was nothing better than having Maya ink his skin—or doing it himself—and letting the needle do its work. He wasn't a pain junkie, far from it if he was honest with himself, but he liked the adrenaline that led the way into fucking fantastic art. While some people thought bodies were sacred and tattoos only marred them, he knew it differently. Art on canvas, any canvas, could have the potential to be art worth bleeding for. As such, he was particular as to who laid a needle on his skin. He only let Maya ink him when he couldn't do it himself. Maya was the same way. Whatever she couldn't do herself, he did.

They were brother and sister, friends, and co-owners of Montgomery Ink.

He and Maya had opened the shop a decade ago when she'd turned twenty. He probably could have opened it a few years earlier since he was eight years older than Maya, but he'd wanted to wait until she was ready. They were joint owners. It had never been his shop while she worked with him. They both had equal say, although with the way Maya spoke, sometimes her voice seemed louder. His deeper one carried just as much weight, even if he didn't yell as much.

Barely.

Sure, he wasn't as loud as Maya, but he got his point across when needed. His voice held control and authority.

He picked up a juice box for Rick from their mini-fridge and turned down the music on his way back. Sloane scowled at him, but the corner of his mouth twitched as if he held back a laugh.

"Thank God one of you has a brain in his head," Maya mumbled in the now quieter room. She rolled her eyes as both he and Sloane flipped her off then went back to her sketch. Yeah, she could have gotten up to turn the music down herself, but then she couldn't have vented her excess energy at the two of them. That was just how his sister worked, and there would be no changing that.

He went back to his station situated in the back so he had the corner space, handed Rick his juice, then rubbed his back. Damn, he was getting old. Thirty-eight wasn't that far up there on the scales, but ever since he'd gotten back from New Orleans, he hadn't been able to shake the weight of something off of his chest.

He needed to be honest. He'd started feeling this way since before New Orleans. He'd gone down to the city to visit his cousin Shep and try to get out of his funk. He'd broken up with

Shannon right before then; however, in reality, it wasn't as much a breakup as a lack of connection and communication. They hadn't cared about each other enough to move on to the next level, and as sad as that was, he was fine with it. If he couldn't get up the energy to pursue a woman beyond a couple of weeks or months of heat, then he knew he was the problem. He just didn't know the solution. Shannon hadn't been the first woman who had ended the relationship in that fashion. There'd been Brenda, Sandrine, and another one named Maggie.

He'd cared for all of them at the time. He wasn't a complete asshole, but he'd known deep down that they weren't going to be with him forever, and they thought the same of him. He also knew that it was time to actually find a woman to settle down with.

If he wanted a future, a family, he was running out of time.

Going to New Orleans hadn't worked out in the least considering, at the time, Shep was falling in love with a pretty blonde named Shea. Not that Austin begrudged the man that. Shep had been his best friend growing up, closer to him than his four brothers and three sisters. It'd helped that he and Shep were the same age while the next of his siblings, the twins Storm and Wes, were four years younger.

His parents had taken their time to have eight kids, meaning he was a full fifteen years older than the baby, Miranda, but he hadn't cared. The eight of them, most of his cousins, and a few strays were as close as ever. He'd helped raise the youngest ones as an older brother but had never felt like he had to. His parents,

Marie and Harry, loved each of their kids equally and had put their whole beings into their roles as parents. Every single concert, game, ceremony, or even parent-teacher meeting was attended by at least one of them. On the good days, the ones where Dad could get off work and Mom had the day off from Montgomery Inc., they both would attend. They loved their kids.

He loved being a Montgomery.

The sound of Sloane's needle buzzing as he sang whatever tune played in his head made Austin grin.

And he fucking *loved* his shop.

Every bare brick and block of polished wood, every splash of black and hot pink—colors he and Maya had fought on and he'd eventually given in to—made him feel at home. He'd taken the family crest and symbol, the large MI surrounded by a broken floral circle, and used it as their logo. His brothers, Storm and Wes, owned Montgomery Inc., a family construction company that their father had once owned and where their mother had worked at his side before they'd retired. They, too, used the same logo since it meant family to them.

In fact, the MI was tattooed on every single immediate family member—including his parents. His own was on his right forearm tangled in the rest of his sleeve but given a place of meaning. It meant Montgomery Iris—*open your eyes, see the beauty, remember who you are*. It was only natural to use it for their two respective companies.

Not that the Ink vs Inc. wasn't confusing as hell, but fuck, they were Montgomerys. They could do whatever they wanted.

As long as they were together, they'd get through it.

Montgomery Ink was just as much his home as his house on the ravine. While Shep had gone on to work at Midnight Ink and created another family there, Austin had always wanted to own his shop. Maya growing up to want to do the same thing had only helped.

Montgomery Ink was now a thriving business in downtown Denver right off 16th Street Mall. They were near parking, food, and coffee. There really wasn't more he needed. The drive in most mornings could suck once he got on I-25, but it was worth it to live out in Arvada. The 'burbs around Denver made it easy to live in one area of the city and work in another. Commutes, though hellish at rush hour, weren't as bad as some. This way he got the city living when it came to work and play, and the option to hide behind the trees pressed up against the foothills of the Rocky Mountains once he got home.

It was the best of both worlds.

At least for him.

Austin got back on his stool and concentrated on Rick's sleeve for another hour before calling it quits. He needed a break for his lower back, and Rick needed a break from the pain. Not that Rick was feeling much since the man currently looked like he'd just gotten laid—pain freaks, Austin loved them—but he didn't want to push either of them too far. Also, Plus Rick's arm had started to swell slightly from all the shading and multiple colors. They'd do another session, the last, hopefully, in a month or so when both of them could work it in their schedules and then finish up.

Austin scowled at the computer at the front of shop, his fingers too big for the damn keys on the prissy computer Maya had demanded they buy.

"Fuck!"

He'd just deleted Rick's whole account because he couldn't find the right button.

"Maya, get your ass over here and fix this. I don't know what the hell I did."

Maya lifted one pierced brow as she worked on a lower back tattoo for some teenage girl who didn't look old enough to get ink in the first place.

"I'm busy, Austin. You're not an idiot, though evidence at the moment points to the contrary. Fix it yourself. I can't help it if you have ape hands."

Austin flipped her off then took a sip of his Coke, wishing he had something stronger considering he hated paperwork. “I was fine with the old keyboard and the PC, Maya. You’re the one who wanted to go with the Mac because it looked pretty.”

“Fuck you, Austin. I wanted a Mac because I like the software.”

Austin snorted while trying to figure out how to find Rick’s file. He was pretty sure it was a lost cause at this point. “You hate the software as much as I do. You hit the damn red X and close out files more than I do. Everything’s in the wrong place, and the keyboard is way too fucking dainty.”

“I’m going to go with Austin on this one,” Sloane added in, his beefy hands in the air.

“See? I’m not alone.”

Maya let out a breath. “We can get another keyboard for you and Gigantor’s hands, but we need to keep the Mac.”

"And why is that?" he demanded.

"Because we just spent a whole lot of money on it, and once it goes, we can get another PC. Fuck the idea that everything can be all in one. I can't figure it out either." She held up a hand. "And don't even think about breaking it. I'll know, Austin. I *always* know."

Austin held back a grin. He wouldn't be surprised if the computer met with an earlier than expected unfortunate fate now that Maya had relented.

Right then, however, that idea didn't help. He needed to find Rick's file.

"Callie!" Austin yelled over the buzz of needles and soft music Maya had allowed them to play.

"What?" His apprentice came out of the break room, a sketchbook in one hand and a smirk on her face. She'd dyed her hair again so it had black and red highlights. It looked good on her, but honestly, he never knew what color she'd have next. "Break something on the computer again with those big man hands?"

"Shut up, minion," he teased. Callie was an up-and-coming artist, and if she kept on the track she was on, he and Maya knew she'd be getting her own chair at Montgomery Ink soon. Not that he'd tell Callie that, though. He liked keeping her on her toes. She reminded him of his little sister Miranda so much that he couldn't help but treat her as such.

She pushed him out of the way and groaned. "Did you have to press *every* button as you rampaged through the operating system?"

Austin could have sworn he felt his cheeks heat, but since he had a thick enough beard, he knew no one would have been able to tell.

Hopefully.

He hated feeling as if he didn't know what he was doing. It wasn't as if he didn't know how to use a computer. He wasn't an idiot. He just didn't know *this* computer. And it bugged the shit out of him.

After a couple of keystrokes and a click of the mouse, Callie stepped back with a smug smile on her face. "Okay, boss, you're all ready to go, and Rick's file is back where it should be. What else do you need from me?"

He bopped her on the head, messing up her red and black hair he knew she spent an hour on every morning with a flat iron. He couldn't help it.

"Go clean a toilet or something."

Callie rolled her eyes. “I’m going to go sketch. And you’re welcome.”

“Thanks for fixing the damn thing. And really, go clean the bathroom.”

“Not gonna do it,” she sang as she skipped to the break room.

“You really have no control over your apprentice,” Sloane commented from his station.

Because he didn’t want that type of control with her. Well, hell, his mind kept going to that dark place every few minutes it seemed.

“Shut up, asshole.”

“I see your vocabulary hasn’t changed much,” Shannon purred from the doorway.

He closed his eyes and prayed for patience. Okay, maybe he’d lied to himself when he said it was mutual and easy to break up with her. The damn woman kept showing up. He didn’t think she wanted him, but she didn't want him to forget her either.

He did not understand women.

Especially this one.

"What do you want, Shannon?" he bit out, needing that drink now more than ever.

She sauntered over to him and scraped her long, red nail down his chest. He'd liked that once. Now, not even a little. They were decent together when they'd dated, but he'd had to hide most of himself from her. She'd never tasted the edge of his flogger or felt his hand on her ass when she'd been bent over his lap. That hadn't been what she wanted, and Austin was into the kind of kink that meant he wanted what he wanted when he wanted. It didn't mean he wanted it every time.

Not that Shannon would ever understand that.

"Oh, baby, you know what I want."

He barely resisted the urge to roll his eyes. As he took a step back, he saw the gleam in her eyes and decided to head it off at the pass. He was in no mood to play her games, or whatever she wanted to do that night. He wanted to go home, drink a beer, and forget this oddly annoying day.

"If you don't want ink, then I don't know what you're doing here, Shannon. We're done." He tried to say it quietly, but his voice was deep, and it carried.

"How could you be so cruel?" She pouted.

"Oh, for the love of God," Maya sneered. "Go home, little girl. You and Austin are through, and I'm pretty sure it was mutual. Oh, and you're not getting any ink here. You're not getting Austin's hands on you this way, and there's no way in hell I'm putting my art on you. Not if you keep coming back to bug the man you didn't really date in the first place."

"Bi—" Shannon cut herself off as Austin glared. Nobody called his sister a bitch. Nobody.

"Goodbye, Shannon." Jesus, he was too old for this shit.

"Fine. I see how it is. Whatever. You were only an okay lay anyway." She shook her ass as she left, bumping into a woman in a linen skirt and blouse.

The woman, whose long honey-brown hair hung in waves down to her breasts, raised a brow. "I see your business has an...interesting clientele."

Austin clenched his jaw. Seriously the wrong thing to say after Shannon.

"If you've got a problem, you can head on right back to where you came from, Legs," he bit out, his voice harsher than he'd intended.

She stiffened then raised her chin, a clear sense of disdain radiating off of her.

Oh yes, he knew who this was, legs and all. Ms. Elder. He hadn't caught a first name. Hadn't wanted to. She had to be in her late twenties, maybe, and owned the soon-to-be-opened boutique across the street. He'd seen her strut around in her too-tall heels and short skirts but hadn't been formally introduced.

Not that he wanted an introduction.

She was too damn stuffy and ritzy for his taste. Not only her store but the woman herself. The look of disdain on her face made him want to show her the door and never let her back in.

He knew what he looked like. Longish dark brown hair, thick beard, muscles covered in ink with a hint of more ink coming out of his shirt. He looked like a felon to some people who didn't know the difference, though he'd never seen the inside of a jail cell in his life. But he knew people like Ms. Elder. They judged people like him. And that one eyebrow pissed him the fuck off.

He didn't want this woman's boutique across the street from him. He'd liked it when it was an old record store. People didn't glare at his store that way. Now he had to walk past the mannequins with the rich clothes and tiny lacy scraps of things if he wanted a fucking coffee from the shop next door.

Damn it, this woman pissed him off, and he had no idea why.

"Nice to meet you too. Callie!" he shouted, his eyes still on Ms. Elder as if he couldn't pull his gaze from her. Her green eyes never left his either, and the uncomfortable feeling in his gut wouldn't go away.

Callie ran up beside him and held out her hand. "Hi, I'm Callie. How can I help you?"

Ms. Elder blinked once. Twice. "I think I made a mistake," she whispered.

Fuck. Now he felt like a heel. He didn't know what it was with this woman, but he couldn't help but act like an ass. She hadn't even done anything but lift an eyebrow at him, and he'd already set out to hate her.

Callie shook her head then reached for Ms. Elder's elbow. "I'm sure you haven't. Ignore the growly, bearded man over there. He needs more caffeine. And his ex was just in here; that alone would make anyone want to jump off the Royal Gorge. So, tell me, how can I help you? Oh! And what's your name?"

Ms. Elder followed Callie to the sitting area with leather couches and portfolios spread over the coffee table and then sat down.

"I'm Sierra, and I want a tattoo." She looked over her shoulder and glared at Austin. "Or, at least, I thought I did."

Austin held back a wince when she turned her attention from him and cursed himself. Well, fuck. He needed to learn not to put his foot in his mouth, but damn it, how was he supposed to know she wanted a tattoo? For all he knew, she wanted to come in there and look down on the place. That was his own prejudice coming into play. He needed to make it up to her. After all, they were neighbors now. However, from the cross look on her face and the feeling in the room, he knew that he wasn't going to be able to make it up to her today. He'd let Callie help her out to start with, and then he'd make sure he was the one who laid ink on her skin.

After all, it was the least he could do. Besides, his hands all of a sudden—or not so suddenly if he really thought about it—wanted to touch that delicate skin of hers and find out her secrets.

Austin cursed. He wouldn't let his thoughts go down that path. She'd break under his care, under his needs. Sure, Sierra Elder might be hot, but she wasn't the woman for him.

If he knew anything, he knew *that* for sure.

An Alpha's Path

**From New York Times Bestselling Author Carrie Ann Ryan's Redwood Pack Series**

Melanie is a twenty-five year old chemist who has spent all of her adult life slaving at school. With her PhD in hand, she's to start her dream job, but before she does, her friend persuades her to relax and try to live again. A blind date set up through her friends seems like the perfect solution. Melanie can take one night away from the lab and let her inner vixen out on a fixed blind date – a chance to get crazy with a perfect stranger. The gorgeous hunk she's to meet exceeds her wildest dreams – but he is more than what he appears and Melanie's analytical mind goes into overdrive.

Kade, a slightly older werewolf (at over one hundred years), needs a night way from the Pack. Too many responsibilities and one near miss with a potential mate made Kade hide in his work, the only peace he can find. His brother convinces him to meet the sexy woman for a one night of fun. What could it hurt? But when he finds this woman could be his mate, can he convince her to leave her orderly, sane world and be with him and his wolf-half, for life?

# Dust of My Wings

**From New York Times Bestselling Author Carrie Ann Ryan's Dante's Circle Series**

*Humans aren't as alone as they choose to believe. Every human possesses a trait of supernatural that lays dormant within their genetic make-up. Centuries of diluting and breeding have allowed humans to think they are alone and untouched by magic. But what happens when something changes?*

Neat freak lab tech, Lily Banner lives her life as any ordinary human. She's dedicated to her work and loves to hang out with her friends at Dante's Circle, their local bar. When she discovers a strange blue dust at work she meets a handsome stranger holding secrets – and maybe her heart. But after a close call with a thunderstorm, she may not be as ordinary as she thinks.

Shade Griffin is a warrior angel sent to Earth to protect the supernaturals' secrets. One problem, he can't stop leaving dust in odd places around town. Now he has to find every ounce of his dust and keep the presence of the supernatural a secret. But after a close encounter with a sexy lab tech and a lightning quick connection, his millennia old loyalties may shift and he could lose more than just his wings in the chaos.

Warning: Contains a sexy angel with a choice to make and a green-eyed lab tech who dreams of a dark-winged stranger. Oh yeah, and a shocking spark that's sure to leave them begging for more.

# Charmed Spirits

**From New York Times Bestselling Author Carrie Ann Ryan's Holiday Montana Series**

Jordan Cross has returned to Holiday, Montana after eleven long years to clear out her late aunt's house, put it on the market, and figure out what she wants to do with the rest of her life. Soon, she finds herself facing the town that turned its back on her because she was different. Because being labeled a witch in a small town didn't earn her many friends...especially when it wasn't a lie.

Matt Cooper has lived in Holiday his whole life. He's

perfectly content being a bachelor alongside his four single brothers in a very small town. After all, the only woman he'd ever loved ran out on him without a goodbye. But now Jordan's back and just as bewitching as ever. Can they rekindle their romance with a town set against them?

Warning: Contains an intelligent, sexy witch with an attitude and drop-dead gorgeous man who likes to work with his hands, holds a secret that might scare someone, and really, *really*, likes table tops for certain activities. Enough said.

Printed in Great Britain
by Amazon

35548958R00132